AFRICA

NII AYIKWEI PARKES is a writer and Senior Editor at flipped eye publishing. A 2007 recipient of Ghana's national ACRAG award for poetry and literary advocacy, he is a former International Writing Fellow at the University of Southampton and author of the acclaimed hybrid novel *Tail of the Blue Bird* (Jonathan Cape, 2009), which has won awards in three countries, including the Prix Laure Bataillon in France. Nii Ayikwei writes for children under the name K. P. Kojo and spends his time in the United Kingdom and in Ghana, where he is director of the Ama Ata Aidoo Centre for Creative Writing.

K. P. KOJO

TALES FROM

AFRICA

Illustrations by JOE LILLINGTON

PUFFIN CLASSICS

PUFFIN BOOKS

UK | USA | Canada | Ireland | Australia
India | New Zealand | South Africa

Puffin Books is part of the Penguin Random House group of companies
whose addresses can be found at global.penguinrandomhouse.com.

www.penguin.co.uk
www.puffin.co.uk
www.ladybird.co.uk

First published 2017
001

Text copyright © K. P. Kojo, 2017
Illustrations by Joe Lillington
Illustrations copyright © Penguin Books Ltd, 2017

The moral right of the author and illustrator has been asserted

Set in 11.5/15 pt Minion
Typeset by Jouve (UK), Milton Keynes
Printed in Great Britain by Clays Ltd, St Ives plc

A CIP catalogue record for this book is available from the British Library

ISBN: 978–0–141–37307–2

All correspondence to
Puffin Books
Penguin Random House Children's
80 Strand, London WC2R 0RL

For all my kiddies, the world's best nieces and nephews:
Omara Okailey, Quinceo Fifi, Della Okaikor, Jerome
Ayitey, Cameron, Jean Ayikailey, Sarah Marie, Carmen
Akuyea, Jodelle Ayikaikor, Jeremiah Kwaku, Leona
Ayikaikai and Yaa Aseda. But especially for my
little editor, NaaNaa.

Contents

Author's Note

Compiling and writing *Tales from Africa* has been a hugely entertaining adventure. A Ghanaian with family roots in the Seychelles, Sierra Leone and beyond, I have friends and family all over the African continent and working on this collection gave me licence to call them and be a questioning child again without shame.

In my early childhood, I often pestered my parents for stories. My impatience for new tales probably fuelled the rapid development of my ability to read. By the age of three, if I wanted a new story I could read one myself.

With hindsight, my fascination with stories is rooted in a desire to know the unknown, to surpass the familiar, to discover the new. I believe that urge exists in all humans to some degree. For that reason, I resist trends towards making stories familiar for readers. What is important, to my mind, is that stories are understandable (not to be confused with familiar), relatable and teach us something new.

Rather than simply retelling very well-known stories from familiar corners of Africa – such as South Africa and

Nigeria – I spoke to friends and family from places like Libya, Madagascar, Angola and Mauritius. Inevitably, kingdoms with strong storytelling traditions such as the Zulu, Akan and Igbo are represented, but I have either found more marginal stories from those traditions, or retold the stories in ways that renew them. For example, the Igbo fable of the tortoise and the birds, made famous by Chinua Achebe, is retold here as 'A Tortoise Named Ununile', incorporating Uri, the Igbo custom of body painting, and making it central to Tortoise's deception. In keeping with the culturally expansive upbringing I had in Accra, I try to respect the place of local traditions and norms in the stories, retaining indigenous names and customs.

There will be words that an untutored tongue might find difficult to pronounce initially, but, as I say whenever I·visit a theatre, library or school to read, every word is made up of small units; if you break it up and put it back together you'll usually get it right.

Ultimately, of the dozens of stories that I read or heard while researching this collection, I decided to retell nine that I absolutely loved. They cover a range of attributes and failings that come into play in all animal (for animals are vital in storytelling) and human life: jealousy, greed, love, forgiveness, ambition, humility, anger, selflessness and grief. Some stories, such as 'The Rebirth of Andriambahoaka' and 'The Frog's Wedding', were completely new to me and it was a real delight to discover them over and over again as

I spoke to more people. It is truly stunning how many versions of each story exist in the communities that share them. It proves that even when we don't know of them, even when they are not widely published or translated, stories continue to live and enrich their communities in new ways.

Because the origins of stories lie in kingdoms that run beyond the borders of what we now recognize as countries, I have largely identified stories by their cultural origin rather than by borders that have come into existence over the last century. I encourage readers to find out about the kingdoms as they have fascinating histories outside of the stories that they used to entertain and teach their citizens. In addition to respecting cultural rather than geographical borders, I have sought to subtly address wildlife and environmental concerns as I reshaped the stories, by highlighting the beauty and harmony of rural life. The Sudan cheetah (*Acinonyx jubatus soemmeringii*) that appears in 'The Cheetah's Whisker', for example, is now listed as a vulnerable species. It once roamed the East African savannah in large numbers. It's a truly magnificent cat that should not be hunted simply to provide pets and pretty foot rugs. It is my hope that its role in the story will encourage more people to get involved in protecting it.

I have had some very important guides and companions during this storytelling journey. For every story I have had to check for versions, corruptions and adaptations – all of which result in great stories in case you were wondering. However, without my international crew of researchers, friends, fellow writers and oral historians, I would never have managed to find the essential starting points for retelling these stories. I would particularly like to thank NoViolet Bulawayo, who pointed me in the direction of Vusamazulu Credo Mutwa's *Indaba My Children: African Folktales* as a research source; Hisham Matar, who connected me to Adam Benkato, a researcher on Libyan *khurafat* (sayings/tales) and currently a Humboldt fellow at Freie Universität Berlin, who provided the bones of 'Um Bsisi's Milk'; Brian Chikwava, who translated some reference material from Zimbabwe for me; North Kaneshie area crew, especially Kofi Oppong, for all the 'tooli' when we were kids; Ian Hussain and Shelina Permalloo for getting me thinking about Mauritius; and Jean Luc Raharimanana, who did the same for Madagascar. Yet, in the end, the stories would not have been as fun to write without my ever-present reader and critic, my daughter NaaNaa, whose frowns and laughter were indispensable editing prompts. She has my unreserved gratitude. Never in the history of literature has an eight-year-old been so powerful.

Finally, of course, I'd like to thank the team at Puffin who have had to endure my erratic bursts of writing and my unyielding defence of names and norms from the African continent. My sincere gratitude to Alex Antscherl, who commissioned me, and to Helen Levene, my editor, who has been as sensitive, open and responsive an editor as one could ever hope for.

I sincerely hope you enjoy these stories, which are but a minute sampling of the thousands of stories that enrich the everyday lives of children and adults across all the countries in Africa. I am proud to share these nine with you in the English language – in print.

The Rebirth of Andriambahoaka

A Sakalava tale

In the days before we were, the days before today, the earth's creatures were all mixed up. You could be a crocodile and a grasshopper – a crochopper, or a snail with the red blood of a lion – a snaion. It was hard to tell what a creature was just by looking, because a snaion, for example, looked just like a snail, although it could roar at night. However, it was possible to tell which creatures stayed on one land – onelanders, and which ones lived on many, as birds do – birdlanders. This tale is about both – a bird with a human heart called Ivorombe and a human king with the eyes of a lemur called Andriambahoaka.

Mother bird, Ivorombe, was a large and unusual bird. She had an orange-red bill that weaved through trees like a flashing light when she passed through a forest. She had white tail streamers that drew loops as she flew, and a streak of pink on her back. Her eyes were particularly striking, with black eye patches over her white feathers that made it look like she was wearing spectacles. Her bill wasn't just colourful, it was big, with a large bottom for storing food and other useful things – a bit like a pelican's bill. In fact, Ivorombe is the grandmother of herons and tropicbirds and pelicans.

One day Ivorombe was flying home from a visit to her cousins in a far-off continent when she felt her eggs grow heavy in her. She needed to lay them right away so that she wouldn't lose them in the ocean. Luckily, there was an island close by and she flew there, swooped around to find a safe place in the forest, far from the humans who lived on the island, and made a strong nest of twigs, grass and leaves.

She laid her eggs, tucked her tail streamers beneath her and sat on them.

For weeks, Ivorombe stayed on top of her eggs. Her body kept them at just the right warm temperature to hatch and she fed herself from food she had stored in the large bottom of her bill.

She had corn.
She had fish.
She had rice.
She had worms.
She had beans, oysters and she had insects.

Each day she would pick two to mix and swallow them from the pouch below her bill. Her favourite mix was beans and fish.

Some days a human would come into the forest to pick from the beautiful flowers that grew there in bursts of purple, orange, indigo, white, red, blue and yellow, or to check traps that they had set to catch meat. Ivorombe would keep very still and silent until the person left, which wasn't easy because she was a very large bird, the size of a human and a bit more. But Ivorombe was not really a singing sort of bird, so she didn't attract too much attention.

Also, the other birds in the forest, who understood Ivorombe's desire to protect her eggs, helped her. They were the singing sorts, a bunch of lively birds who had the kind of music and chatter that humans tried to catch and hold on to: rainbow cockatoos, green finches, chameleon parrots, violet vangas, moon-bright starlings and four-toned flufftails. One of the birds, a beepoe, became good friends with Ivorombe and some evenings the odd couple would natter until the moon framed the small beepoe sitting on the shoulder of Ivorombe, who remained unmoving on her eggs. The beepoe was Ivorombe's main source of news. That was because he was a flittering sort – in fact he was the grandfather of the hummingbird. The beepoe was really a hoopoe with the muscles of a bee and he loved sucking nectar from the abundant flowers close to where humans lived. As he flittered he gathered both nectar and news.

It was the beepoe who told Ivorombe that the island she had laid her eggs on was ruled by a king called Andriambahoaka. He had been a good ruler, but he had no children. Almost all the young women on the island had been married to him before but, when no children were forthcoming, after a while they left him. The strange thing was that when they married other men they had children in no time. So the old women now said that Andriambahoaka was cursed and they tried to keep their daughters from him, but because of his liquid lemur eyes nobody could say no when he stared at them. The gold ring that ran around the pitch black of his pupils seemed to contain a spell that caused people to do his bidding.

Weeks later, two of Ivorombe's eggs hatched, but the third did not. When it showed no signs of cracking, it was the beepoe who suggested that something should be done.

'You need to leave the third egg so you can care for the

two chicks,' said the beepoe. 'If you stay there, the two babies you have will die, and we don't know if that last one will hatch.'

'Well, if I *don't* sit on this it won't hatch.'

'What if it takes too long?'

Ivorombe was quiet, her bright bill tucked against her wing.

'You need another bird to sit on this one,' said the beepoe.

'It might hatch in two days.'

'You need a big bird – one that can cover the egg properly.'

'I'm sure it will hatch in two days,' insisted Ivorombe.

'What if it doesn't? These two will starve; you don't have enough food left in your bill.'

The bird friends pondered in silence until the sky darkened and the crickets and crochoppers started their sawing and whistling. It would take the beepoe four days to fly to Ivorombe's land to ask one of her family to come and sit with the egg. With one of Ivorombe's kind, coming back would take two days. That was four days to go and two to come back, making six days – but six days was too much.

'I have an idea,' said the beepoe. 'We can pay a human to do it.'

'A human?!'

'Yes, a human. A human will be big enough to sit on the egg.'

'But won't they destroy it like they destroy everything?'

'They won't if you pay them. I know of a good maiden.'

'But what can I pay with?'

'The pearls left in your bill from eating oysters. Humans like those. We can pay with those.'

Ivorombe was not completely sure, but she felt she had no choice. She counted fifteen pearls and gave them to the beepoe.

There was a woman from the village who could sit on the egg for Ivorombe. She was one of four maidens on the island who had not been married to King Andriambahoaka before. This was because she was short and the king's lemur eyes could not look down, so he had never noticed her. Her name was Iangoria. The beepoe knew her because she had been kind to him once when he was injured near the village. She was skilled at counting backwards, balancing, wrestling, weaving, climbing, catapult shooting and running. Her ability in climbing and balancing made her a perfect caretaker for Ivorombe's egg, as the mother bird's nest was high up on the largest ebony tree for miles.

As soon as Iangoria arrived in the forest with the beepoe, she tied her hair into five tufts on top of her head, climbed to the top of the tree and took over from Ivorombe. While Iangoria was on the egg, Ivorombe fed her two other chicks and flew them over to her land.

When after four days the egg still hadn't hatched, Iangoria began to feed on the ebony tree's jackalberry fruits, which were sweet and filling.

On the seventh day, while talking to the beepoe, Iangoria heard a *crack* . . .

She shifted off the egg a little and saw a clear zigzag line in the shell. The beepoe hovered excitedly, flapping his wings faster and faster.

There was a second *crack* . . .

Then a *cry* . . .

Iangoria tilted her head and the beepoe slowed his wings down, because the cry sounded like a human cry. The maiden crawled away from the egg, stood in the nest, and watched as a human baby girl, the darkest, most beautiful, chubby baby girl, emerged from the egg.

Iangoria rushed forward and picked her up, wiping the egg white off the baby's body, while clasping her with her strong climbing hands. The beepoe fluttered around them, checking to see if the baby had any feathers or wings, or if her mouth looked anything like a beak. The baby cried louder and louder until Iangoria held her close to her breast. She stopped crying and placed a five-fingered hand on Iangoria's chest.

'Maybe she's fully human because you hatched her,' said the beepoe.

Iangoria looked up. 'What will her mother do?'

The beepoe flitted from left to right. 'I don't know. She can't fly . . . A bird's baby that can't fly is a problem . . . We'll just have to wait for Ivorombe.'

When Ivorombe did not return that evening, Iangoria

fed the baby from her own breast. The next day the beepoe helped Iangoria build a platform lower down the ebony tree to protect the baby from the sun.

The platform became the baby's home. The beepoe made her a blanket from elephant grass and Iangoria wove a strong bed from bamboo shoots. They took turns foraging food from the jungle for the baby. They fed her baobab pap, hibiscus nectar, red bananas and a drink made from four o'clock flowers and coconut water, which helps with singing.

Ivorombe's journey back home took longer than she expected. By the time she had settled the two hatched chicks and introduced them to her family, two weeks had passed. When she returned, her third child was already sitting and imitating the songs of warblers and violet vangas. Ivorombe was, of course, stunned, astounded, astonished – she was stun-stoun-dished! But the baby smiled and sheltered under her wing immediately.

'She will be called Imaitsoanala,' said Ivorombe proudly. 'She is my heart come alive.'

The giant bird turned to Iangoria. 'Since she cannot fly I would like you to be her companion and look after her when I am away.'

Iangoria nodded. She had already fallen in love with baby Imaitsoanala and would have stayed to look after her even if Ivorombe was not giving her pearls as a reward.

The beepoe excitedly flitted back and forth, left and right. 'One big family,' he chirped.

Imaitsoanala grew fast on the ebony tree platform. Her mother taught her to hunt and weave and how to land safely when jumping from a great height. When she got jealous of the perfect-pitch singing of the green finches, Ivorombe told her not to get jealous; 'You learn from creatures that are better than you,' she told her. 'Jealousy doesn't teach you anything.'

From Iangoria, Imaitsoanala learned wrestling, counting, climbing, clothes-making, balancing and running. From the beepoe she learned about all the poisonous fruits to avoid in the forest, and how to sow seeds and help plants grow better. By the time she was twelve, she was as much part of the forest as the orchids that clung to the tops of the high trees. Her mother, Ivorombe, came and went every six weeks and every so often she brought Imaitsoanala's bird brother and sister from the other two eggs to visit. But she loved Imaitsoanala fiercely and each time she left her behind she would say to Iangoria: 'Keep her away from people, please. I don't want her to be taken from me.'

One afternoon, when Ivorombe was away, King Andriambahoaka was walking through the forest when he saw Imaitsoanala gathering sweet hibiscus juice with the beepoe. He stopped in his tracks, fascinated by her radiant beauty and carefree smile.

'Whose child is this?' he asked, turning to face his servants.

'*Whose child is this?*' bellowed one of the servants.

As the question echoed through the forest, Iangoria, who was close by, rushed to the clearing. She fell on her knees when she recognized the king.

'My chief, her mother is away, but I am her caretaker.'

'Who is speaking to me?' said Andriambahoaka, whose lemur eyes could not look below his belly.

'There is a woman at your feet, my chief,' said one of his servants.

Andriambahoaka dropped to his knees to address Iangoria. 'This girl is dark and plump and has the most amazing smile I have ever seen. Never have I seen a girl so beautiful. I must have her as my bride.'

Iangoria shook her head. 'My chief, I plead with you to let this girl be. Her mother is the fierce hunting bird Ivorombe, and she would fly into the most destructive rage if she even knew that the girl has been near people. Please let her be.'

'But she is so beautiful,' said Andriambahoaka, fixing Iangoria with his golden gaze.

'If you must, my chief,' said Iangoria. 'But she is not of age now. Come back when she is old enough and speak to her mother.'

*

Andriambahoaka returned to his palace and, for the next few years, spoke of no other thing more than he spoke of the beauty of Imaitsoanala, the girl he was going to marry:

> She had hair shaped like the setting sun
> Her smell was that of the finest musk
> She was the shade of the dark of dusk
> Her smile was as playful as a lion cub
> She was as plump as a young baobab
> Her skin was the texture of silk
> She had teeth the colour of coconut milk
> Her voice was like the starling's song . . .

He spoke of her so much and with so much love that he won the blessing of all his subjects to go and get permission to marry Imaitsoanala when she was of age. Even his two wives agreed, but it was because they wanted to see this girl that Andriambahoaka could not stop talking about.

Andriambahoaka and his servants returned to the forest, bearing gifts. There was gold cloth and soft fruit, beadwork and silver, rice and corn and beans. Andriambahoaka marched towards the giant ebony tree to speak to Ivorombe and ask for Imaitsoanala's hand in marriage.

When he got to the tree Ivorombe was away. Iangoria,

too, had gone with the beepoe to collect hibiscus nectar. Alone on the platform, weaving a new cover for their grain store, was Imaitsoanala.

Andriambahoaka couldn't help himself. 'My sunshine, my dusk, my beautiful flower, I have waited for this day for years. I am hopelessly in love with you. Will you be my bride?'

Imaitsoanala looked towards the sky to see if her mother was on her way home. 'My chief, thank you for your kind words. I am very flattered, but I think it would be better for you to forget about me.'

'I can't forget you,' protested Andriambahoaka, just as Iangoria returned.

Iangoria climbed on to the platform so that the king could see her. 'Why are you speaking to her? I pleaded with you to let her be.'

'I can't,' said the king. 'My love, you must come with me.'

'My chief, you must let me be. My mother will tear you to pieces if you run off with me. Besides, what king wants a bird of prey for a mother-in-law?'

Andriambahoaka shook his head. 'I fear nothing, sweet maiden. My love for you is so strong that I fear nothing.' He stared at her with his deep lemur eyes.

Iangoria tried to plead with the king some more. 'My chief, please wait until her mother returns. I do not feel good about this. Please wait.'

'I can wait no longer.' He held Imaitsoanala's hand. 'Can we go?'

So Ivorombe returned to find her daughter gone. She flew into a fiery rage and set off after Andriambahoaka and his servants. But they had prepared a distraction for her. Along the route away from the ebony tree, the servants had scattered the rice and corn and beans that they had carried as gifts in many different directions.

Ivorombe, who could no longer tell which way they had gone and didn't like to waste food, collected the grains and returned home.

She was furious. She sat up in the ebony tree and cried, heartbroken that her daughter, her heart, could desert her like that. She cried and cried until she was calm. The beepoe flew up to join her and they talked late into the night. Maybe it wasn't so bad that her daughter, Imaitsoanala, was getting married. She was, after all, human.

However, the next day, when Ivorombe visited the palace, she saw her daughter already trying on wedding dresses and weaving a headdress. She flapped her wings in anger. 'I taught you how to weave,' she said – again and again – as she pecked at her own daughter. 'Have you forgotten me already?'

She flayed Imaitsoanala's skin and plucked out her eyes. Still fuming, she flew away with the skin and eyes and hung them on the platform where Imaitsoanala had grown up. Her daughter was left skinless and eyeless.

At the palace, King Andriambahoaka had been waiting to present Imaitsoanala to the people, but only as his bride. He wanted to unveil her at their wedding. However, after Ivorombe had taken her dark skin and eyes, it was painful for Imaitsoanala to go out into the sun, so Andriambahoaka built a special shadowed chamber to protect her. He visited her every day; they spoke for hours and hours. He told her everything he had been taught about his kingdom and she taught him all she knew about birdsongs, making beautiful harmonies with her voice that echoed in the corridors of the palace. Sometimes he carried a tray of red, black and green berries, wore a blindfold and played guess the berry games with her.

Andriambahoaka's two wives were jealous. They had been stunned by how beautiful Imaitsoanala was when she arrived, but now she was skinless and eyeless. She was just a bag of bones. They did not understand why Andriambahoaka was still spending so much time with such an ugly thing.

They bullied Imaitsoanala.

'Until you are married to Andriambahoaka you are just an ordinary person – a servant! You will have to do exactly what we ask you to do.'

They deliberately ran their clothes through mud and gave them to her to wash. They made her scrub the kitchen floors even though they knew she could not see.

Imaitsoanala did all these chores without complaining. 'I'm learning new things,' she said to herself.

But when they gave her the thinnest reeds in the land and asked her to weave large baskets, she cried inside. She could not see. She pricked her hands on the reeds until they bled.

Ivorombe noticed the puddles forming around her daughter's hanging eyes and felt really sorry for the way she had treated Imaitsoanala. She had been too angry. She had punished her too much.

'I should go to her,' she said to Iangoria and the beepoe.

They smiled and nodded. They had been too scared to tell her that they thought she had been very cruel to her daughter.

Ivorombe found Imaitsoanala on the floor of her special shadowed chamber in the palace. She was surrounded by reeds and she was sobbing.

Ivorombe embraced her daughter 'I am sorry, my child, I was unfair. You are human and I should let you live as humans live if you choose. I will return your skin.'

She took the reeds from her daughter and sat beside her. In no time she had finished weaving the baskets and Imaitsoanala took eight perfect large baskets to Andriambahoaka's two wives. The wives were shocked! When they were alone, they turned the baskets this way and that, looking for flaws that they could complain about.

There were none. They had done all they could to upset Imaitsoanala and she was still there with them in the palace. She had not run back to the forest where she belonged.

'We need to do more,' they said.

They marched to Andriambahoaka's chamber and confronted him. 'Our chief,' they pleaded, 'we both love the young girl that you have brought into the palace, but it's been weeks now. It is not right for her to stay on in the palace if you are not going to marry her. The people will start to talk.'

'You are right,' said Andriambahoaka.

'You should marry her right away. It's the best thing. We can help arrange the wedding,' they said, giggling.

Andriambahoaka didn't want to agree because he didn't want a skinless and eyeless Imaitsoanala to have to remove her veil outside. In the hot sun. In front of all those people. But he had no choice. His wives were right. It was the correct thing to do.

He was upset all day and he told Imaitsoanala when he went to see her in the shadowed chamber. He suggested that they get married in two days, touching her skinless hand gently so he would not hurt her.

She smiled. She didn't tell him that her mother was hiding in the room, but she soothed him. 'All is well, my chief. I want to marry you. I will be there.'

Ivorombe got to work immediately. She flew out of Imaitsoanala's window at night and returned with Iangoria and the beepoe. She replaced Imaitsoanala's skin and eyes carefully and the beepoe prepared special herb and flower mixtures for Imaitsoanala to rub over her body. Iangoria wove a gold toga and Ivorombe made the most delicate veil of white and gold to cover her daughter's head.

The beepoe flittered back and forth taking measurements so that the clothes would fit perfectly. He braided the dandelion-shaped hair on Imaitsoanala's head so that it went down her back in tidy cornrows.

On the day of the wedding, Andriambahoaka waited nervously for Imaitsoanala to arrive. He stood on a large platform by the palace steps. In front of him a huge crowd cheered. They were waiting to see the beauty their king had spoken of for so long. The one he said had:

> Hair shaped like the setting sun
> The smell of the finest musk
> A shade the dark of dusk
> A smile as playful as a lion cub
> Flesh as plump as a young baobab
> Skin the texture of silk
> Teeth the colour of coconut milk
> And a voice like the starling's song.

Behind Andriambahoaka, his two wives sneered. They were tired of sharing their good-looking husband with

Imaitsoanala. They could not wait for all the people to see the skinless and eyeless bag of bones they had been living with. They had already told many of their friends, but no one believed them because the king was known always to tell the truth.

The crowd gasped as Imaitsoanala appeared from the side of the palace, guided by Iangoria. They had never seen clothes so radiant, so well made! They watched as she walked unsteadily to stand in front of Andriambahoaka.

He lifted the veil slowly, not caring if all the people thought he was mad for being in love with a skinless woman. But when he flicked the veil back, he was stunned to see the old Imaitsoanala – with skin, with eyes, with a huge smile – staring back at him. He embraced her and kissed her immediately, unable to contain his joy.

The crowd was silent. Imaitsoanala's radiance was unlike anything they had seen before. Ivorombe flew over the gathering, her large shadow giving them a moment's relief from the glaring sun. Everyone looked up, then back at their king, Andriambahoaka, and at Imaitsoanala, then they applauded wildly. She was a perfect bride for their king.

And they were right. Unlike his other wives, whose hearts had turned to stone because of jealousy, Imaitsoanala bore a son. He was named after his father, Andriambahoaka, and grew up to become the greatest ruler the island had ever had.

The Jackal and the Lion

A Khoi and San tale

There was a time when the lion and the jackal were firm friends. Indeed it is no accident that they both like to crouch low. It is a habit they developed in childhood when hunting together in thick plains of lovegrass. Jackal would go ahead, find the prey – some idle eland or zebra – and signal Lion.

Lion would crouch a little distance behind Jackal, waiting for the right moment. When he got the signal, he would run, take a leap off Jackal's back, making an arc like a rainbow, and land – *BAM!* – right on top of the eland or zebra with his claws, and Jackal would laugh, rolling around in circles.

That was Jackal and Lion – perfect hunting partners. No animal wanted to live close to where they heard Jackal and Lion roamed, but Jackal was so cunning that the animals never knew where he was going to be next. He moved all the time: on lowlands, by drying streams, up hills, under the large tree where the giraffes now like to eat, in caves or by the big watering hole that looked like a bruise on the land. There was even said to be a mountain where he stayed sometimes. And wherever Jackal was, chances were that you would find Lion too. And when they were together, there was hunting, there was laughter. They were perfect hunting partners.

But any of the animals will tell you that the days of Jackal and Lion's friendship were the worst days in our kingdom. They hunted so much that Jackal's back turned black from the bruises left by Lion using him as a springboard to pounce on prey.

Lion and his family grew big and strong, their coats glistening and streaked with gold. Jackal, on the other hand, didn't look strong and healthy. In fact, the whole jackal community looked lean and hungry. Their teeth were permanently bared, just waiting for more food from Jackal's hunting, but each time Jackal returned home he only had entrails for them.

It's true, Jackal and Lion were a great hunting team, but Lion was lousy at sharing. He had been like that since they were school cubs, but Jackal was only little then so it didn't matter. Even when Jackal's older brother told him to be careful he took no notice. If Lion didn't share the guinea fowl they caught together, Jackal's mother was at home to give him a piece of her zebra. However, she always warned him, 'Jackal, friends who won't share are not real friends. Watch your back, my son.'

Jackal loved hunting with Lion so then he had simply laughed, but now that he was fully grown and had to hunt for everyone, the whole community could see how much Lion cheated him. They were not happy.

'You can't let all of us starve because your friend does not know how to share,' they said. 'Put an end to it or find somewhere else to live.'

Even Jackal's wife said the same and, for once, Jackal, who was very much a laughing jackal, was upset.

One sundown, when the bush was quiet, Jackal spoke to Lion about the unfair nature of their sharing. Lion guffawed and slapped Jackal's back.

'Look, my friend, what we have is perfect; you are lean and slight, you slide in the grasses beautifully and you signal me. I am big, heavy and *very* strong.' Lion rose on his hind legs and roared, waving his body in the air and startling Jackal, who cowered under his friend's shadow.

'One swipe from my claw and the prey is dead. That is the real hard work. It is only fair that I keep the lion's share. The entrails are just right for keeping you in the best shape for your job, and the sweet flesh keeps me strong so I can do mine.'

Jackal drew a wobbly line in the red sand with his paw. 'But entrails aren't as good for you as the sweet flesh and the fat.'

'Exactly,' said Lion. 'They are no good for me.'

'I mean they are no good for me either, Lion.'

Lion turned to face Jackal with an ear-splitting roar. 'Are you calling me a liar?'

'No.'

'Are you saying that I'm stupid?'

Jackal looked down, shading his eyes from the last burn of the orange sun. 'No, my friend,' he said, as he slowly gathered the entrails from their hunt and went back to his community.

When Jackal got home and delivered the contents of his skin bag, a miserly spread of eland entrails, for dinner, the other jackals turned on him.

There was howling.
There was hooting.
There was catcalling.
There was whistling.

There was booing.

And, finally, there was shooing.

Jackal was cast out of the community to roam by himself.

Now, if you know anything about jackals, you know that jackals roam in packs. A jackal without a pack, without a family, is a miserable jackal – a sad, sad creature. Jackal slunk from cave to elephant grass, to stream, to hill, to lovegrass – all over the kingdom – all alone, thinking of how to get back into his pack.

Lion, meanwhile, was at home feasting on juicy eland with his wife and many cubs.

On their next hunt, down near the big watering hole, Jackal spotted a young zebra. It was separated from its group and was exploring in the grass near a bouquet of pheasants. The silly zebra didn't even look up as the birds took off, sensing danger. With Jackal in place, Lion ran from behind, stepped on his friend's back and jumped high. He swiped the zebra's head with his left claw as he landed on him, then he sank his teeth into the zebra's neck until it was still. The other zebra scattered towards the setting sun.

Jackal laughed and laughed.

'What a stupid zebra,' he cackled. 'How can you be at a watering hole and not look around?' He rolled about in the pale grass. 'A zebra should watch its back.'

But as Lion dragged the zebra towards the lair where they shared their hunts, Jackal fell silent.

'What's the matter, my friend?' asked Lion.

'Well, zebra is my mother's favourite meat. It would be nice to take her some.'

Lion laughed. 'But, of course, you will have a nice bag of entrails for her when we have shared this zebra.'

'No,' said Jackal.

'No? Why?' asked Lion. 'Do you not want your share?'

'Oh, I do,' insisted Jackal, 'but I can't take it back because I've been thrown out of the community.'

'How silly of them. Aren't you the one who takes food to them?' Lion stopped in his tracks and tapped Jackal on the shoulder. 'You mean you have nowhere to go?'

Jackal nodded slowly.

'Ho,' laughed Lion. 'That's great. You can help me by carrying this zebra. Come with me and eat with the lions.'

'Really?'

'Yes, really. Come with me.'

Jackal picked up the zebra and followed Lion. He was happy to have company. If only the jackals who said Lion was only using him could see him now. He was going to eat like a lion – juicy zebra meat to fill his belly. He was going to eat at the lion homestead. Jackal had a smile as wide as the moon.

When Lion's wife served the zebra, she placed large chunks of flesh in front of Lion and all six of his cubs. Jackal's mouth watered as she came to him. His portion seemed as big as Lion's and Jackal shuffled to make space for it in front of him as she set it down. He closed his eyes in anticipation of the feast of flesh and fat, but when he opened them he saw that she had put three huge knots of entrails in front of him.

Jackal glared at Lion, who was already licking his lips after his first morsel. 'I thought you said I would eat like a lion.'

Lion growled. 'Don't interrupt me when I'm eating! You are sitting with lions, aren't you?'

'But . . .'

'Arghh,' roared Lion. 'Don't try my patience. I've told you before, flesh and fat are not good for jackals. Entrails are what you like and they are good for you.'

Jackal shut his mouth. He realized his mother had been right all along. Lion would never be good at sharing. First *he*, Jackal, found the prey, then Lion jumped off *his* back to make the kill, and it was *he* who had even carried the zebra home for Lion today – but still his friend would not share. Now Lion was telling him what jackals liked to eat. How cheeky! Does a lion know what a jackal's stomach feels like? Has a lion ever spent a day in a jackal's skin?

On their next few hunts, Jackal noticed that Lion stopped carrying the meat altogether and instead spent time playfully chasing pheasants and guinea fowls, and rollicking in shallow ponds and clumps of ticklish dwarf grass. Jackal often had to wait for Lion to catch up. Still, when they got back to Lion's homestead, everyone would have the tastiest chunks of the flesh and fat that Jackal had carried, while Jackal was given the knotted entrails.

He always ate in silence, wishing for a day when he would be able to teach Lion a lesson.

One day, soon after the September rains that made the earth on the plains soft and easy to creep on, Jackal and Lion tracked and killed a quagga. Quagga was a kind of zebra that was especially delicious near the hind legs where it had no stripes.

Lion was happy.
Lion was ecstatic.
Lion was joyful.
Lion was enthralled.

Lion was as jumpy as a grasshopper on a hot stone. He lunged at birds here and there, rearing on his hind legs and roaring. He rolled in clumps of ticklish dwarf grass and, because of the rains, he found a pond in which he could almost completely cover himself with sun-warmed water. Lion shook his mane and tried to catch water droplets on his tongue.

Jackal, carrying the quagga alone, stood and waited while his friend played. He glared at Lion until Lion stopped for a moment.

'Oh, Jackal, my friend, you know the way home now. You go on ahead. Give the meat to my wife and I'll join you later.'

'Fine,' said Jackal, annoyed to see his friend already playing back in the water. He set off, pulling the quagga behind him.

As soon as Jackal was a safe distance from Lion, he changed direction and went to the lair where they usually split their hunt. He carved the quagga carefully, putting fat and flesh in one skin bag and the entrails and bones in another.

He threw one heavy skin bag over his shoulder and set off for Lion's homestead. At the gate he greeted Lion's wife and left the skin bag with her.

'Won't you be eating with us tonight?' she asked.

'Not tonight, Mrs Lion, but I'll come tomorrow if Lion is here.'

And with that Jackal was gone. He went back for the other skin bag and went to the mountain, where, because of its many caves, the jackals stayed during times of rain.

As Jackal emerged from the narrow hole that opened on to the trail up the mountain, a few jackal cubs spotted him and ran off to inform the elders. By the time Jackal got to the settlement there was quite a crowd waiting for him, with his frail mother and his older brother right in front.

There was howling.
There was hooting.
There was catcalling.
There was whistling.
There was booing.

But they did not shoo him away. The jackals were hungry and they had noticed that Jackal was carrying something heavy behind him.

'We hope you have not brought more entrails with you, because if you have you can turn right round and go back to your friend Lion.'

Jackal smiled. He put down the skin bag and reached for the juiciest piece of quagga hind leg. Then he removed it, sprang to his mother and gave it to her. 'Your favourite, mother. Not just zebra, but quagga zebra.'

There was cheering.
There was clapping.
There was backslapping.
There was laughing.
There was dancing.
And finally there was eating.

The jackals had just about finished eating when they heard a thunderous roar from the foot of the mountain.

The young cubs cowered and slunk into caves and spaces beneath rocks.

But Jackal wasn't scared at all. He knew that Lion, after all his years of eating fat and flesh, could not fit through the hole that led to the trail up the mountain.

'Gireb!' Lion roared from below.

Gireb was Jackal's school name and only his teachers had used it. It was a sign that Lion was furious.

Jackal smiled and leaned over the edge of the mountain. 'Ah, Lion, my dear friend and advisor . . . my mentor, even!'

'Don't call me advisor, don't call me mentor,' said Lion. 'You gave my family entrails to eat and you dare call me *mentor*?'

'Entrails?' yelped Jackal, feigning shock. 'It's not possible.'

'I said you gave my family entrails,' roared Lion.

'It's not possible,' insisted Jackal. 'The quagga was heavy so I got my brother to help me carry it here, but I cut it up myself. I put all the flesh and fat in one skin bag for you and all the entrails and bones in another skin bag for me. When I finished, I just turned away for a minute to clean my coat, then I asked my brother to pass me the skin bag. I took the bag directly to Mrs Lion myself.'

'You gave *my* family entrails!' Lion repeated.

Jackal looked at Lion over the ledge and scratched his ear.

'Lion, old friend, forgive me. I think I've realized what happened. My brother gave me the wrong skin bag.'

Lion growled. 'But that will not feed my family. Where is the flesh?'

'He is very sorry, Lion. I am just going to tell him off severely right now.'

Jackal moved from the edge of the mountain and pretended to shout at his brother for being so foolish.

Jackal returned to the ledge. 'He is seriously sorry, Lion. It won't happen again.'

'But, even so, I have only had entrails for dinner.'

'Well, old friend, there is still some flesh and fat up here – not enough for all your family, but why don't you come up here and eat your fill? I won't tell them.'

'You know I won't fit through that passage to come up,' Lion growled.

'Don't worry. I'll throw you a rope. My jackal community will help you up.'

And so the jackals wove a nice, strong rope with vines and threw it down to Lion. Lion tied it round his narrow waist and the jackals pulled him upwards.

But . . .

Just as Lion got to the ledge . . .

Jackal signalled to them to let go and Lion fell with a thud – *BAM!* – just like when he landed on prey.

'Arghhh!' Lion roared.

'So sorry. So sorry, my friend. My stupid brother let go of the rope!'

'I'm sore . . .' groaned Lion.

'Really,' said Jackal, 'let me deal with my brother again. This time I will beat him for his carelessness.'

Jackal left the ledge and pretended to beat his brother by hitting the empty skin bag with a stick. The jackal's brother screamed so loud that even Lion cried out for Jackal to stop.

'It's enough,' he said. 'Can you pull me up to eat? More carefully this time.'

'OK,' said Jackal, winking at his friends.

So the jackals took hold of the rope again and heaved Lion up. This time they pulled him quite far up – enough for his whiskers to touch the top. He was suddenly face to face with his friend Jackal, close enough to whisper to him.

Lion smelled the delicious quagga flesh and smiled, but as he lifted his claws to grip the edge of the mountain, the jackals let go of the rope.

Jackal pretended he was trying to catch the rope as Lion fell, then he ran back to help his brother beat the skin bag again.

Lion heard the screaming from the foot of the mountain, where he had fallen flat on his back. 'Stop it,' he groaned.

Jackal rushed to look down. 'What did you say, my friend?'

'I said, stop it. It's not his fault. You jackals are too weak to lift a lion.'

Lion rolled on to his front and stood tall, shaking the dust off his coat in spite of the severe aches and pains from his two falls. 'Say, old friend,' he said, 'that quagga flesh smells wonderful.'

'It is, Lion. I'm surprised that we jackals have preferred *entrails* for such a long time.'

Lion laughed. 'Gireb, you are teasing me. I explained to you; it is for the jobs we do. For example, if I do not have flesh and fat, I may not be as strong when we hunt tomorrow. Then we will both starve.'

'Oh, Lion! Jackals never starve. We have been around for thousands of years. But I understand that you need some fat and flesh tonight. Why don't I throw some down to you?'

'You would do that for me, Jackal?'

'Of course, old friend, of course. Why don't you open your mouth and let us throw the pieces in?'

Lion settled on his hindquarters, lifted his magnificent head to the sky and opened his jaws to their fullest width.

Up on the mountain Jackal and his family collected rocks, wrapped them in quagga skin and rubbed them with leftover fat. When they had nine pieces, they stacked them at the edge of the mountain.

'Are you ready, Lion?' Jackal shouted.

'Yes,' roared Lion impatiently. 'Can't you see?'

'OK, I have ten pieces for you. Here comes the first.'

Jackal threw the first rock directly into Lion's throat, near the back of the tongue, where Lion would taste the sweet fat first.

Lion didn't even try to chew. He just swallowed the rock, delighted to feel its weight settle in his belly.

'Do you want the next one?' shouted Jackal cheerily.

'Yes,' growled Lion. 'Make it quick.'

Jackal threw the second rock down, then the third.

Lion paused to lick his lips. 'This quagga is quite heavy, Jackal,' he said.

'Yes, Lion. This quagga is very special. I have seven pieces left. Should I pack them for you to take to your wife and six cubs?' asked Jackal, to see if Lion would want to share with his own family.

'No. I'm not full yet. Throw down the next piece.' Lion opened his jaws again.

Jackal tossed the next piece into Lion's throat.

And then another.

And then another.

After the sixth piece, Lion couldn't stomach any more. He felt the weight of his belly becoming hard for him to support. Still, he wanted to finish the meat, so he asked Jackal to wait for a moment so he could settle his stomach. Lion would have stayed at the foot of the mountain all night if that is what it took, but Jackal did not want his old friend to be so close when he realized that he had been tricked. He would be able to call the attention of other lions to the jackals' hiding place.

'Lion,' Jackal said. 'Why don't you go home and sleep it off? I will keep the rest for you to come and finish tomorrow.'

Lion lifted his head. 'That's a great idea, my friend. I'll see you tomorrow for the hunt.'

Well, I can tell you that Lion didn't turn up for the hunt the next day. See, while a Lion has very wide jaws, its bum is no bigger than a goat's – and those rocks had to come out somehow. In the middle of the night, Lion was heard all across the kingdom wailing in pain as those rocks taught him a lesson about greed and the importance of sharing.

Soon the other animals came back to the kingdom in greater numbers and the giraffes returned to the large tree where they once gathered.

Lion must have told his cubs what happened before he died because, when you see lions feeding these days, they always test the meat with their claws first and they almost always let it fall to the ground first.

And jackals? Jackals watch their backs. They are careful to stay behind lions, just in case some young lion decides to pay them back for greedy Lion's rock supper.

The Frog's Wedding

An M'baka and Ambundu tale

There was once a young cattle herder named Itanda. He was wealthy and strong, and his cattle were healthy, but he spent hours every day just staring at the sky. Every single day.

'If my cattle were up there,' he'd say, 'it would be so easy to keep an eye on them.'

In fact, he talked about the sky so much that one day a passing parrot stopped to challenge him: 'If you think the sky is so perfect, why don't you go and live in the Sky Kingdom?'

Itanda thought about it for a moment, then he answered. 'Maybe I will!'

However, living in the Sky Kingdom wasn't so easy to do. The Sky Chief had to give you permission and teach you how to climb the invisible spiderweb ladder that led to the kingdom. He only gave permission to creatures that were useful to the kingdom.

If you were good at arranging clouds, or supervising suns and moons to make sure they went to bed at the right time, the Sky Chief would invite you at once. Also, because the Sky Kingdom was always losing water as rain, they needed many people to fetch water from Earth daily. Otherwise you had to be married to a citizen of the kingdom.

There were seven maidens from the Sky Chief's own homestead who came from the heavens each day to fetch water for everyone who lived there. Although no one from Earth was allowed to speak to them, everyone had heard them gossiping about the Sky Chief's warrior wife and their brilliant and beautiful daughter, who was unmarried.

Since Itanda had no special skills that would be useful to the Sky Kingdom, he decided that the Sky Chief's daughter would have to be his bride. He sat on a rock and composed a letter to the Sky Chief:

> I, Itanda, cattle herder of renown,
> a man made of soil's rich brown,

a walker of plains and hills high,
wish to make your daughter my wife.

He was very happy with the letter, but he needed someone to help him deliver it. As he couldn't ask the seven maidens who fetched water daily at the deep forest well, Itanda roamed between the trees and in the thick undergrowth, looking for anyone else who was close to heaven.

He asked the giraffe because her neck was **so long**. (Giraffe said no because she could only carry things as far as her head went. 'That's not close to heaven!') So he asked the rabbit because his hind legs were **so strong**. (But Rabbit said he could only really hop as high as Giraffe's belly. 'That's not close to heaven!') Next, Itanda asked the bald eagle because he swooped in the sky and the soko antelope because she could jump so high . . .
    NO.
Neither of them could get his letter to heaven. So he asked the colobus monkey because he could climb to incredible heights . . .
    NO.
Monkey said he could only reach as high as the highest tree, which looked like it reached heaven from the middle of the forest, but that was just

something called *perspective* and it was not *at all* close to heaven.

By evening, a tired Itanda went to ask the striped hyena if she would read the letter out to the heavens as she howled so loudly at night.

Hyena didn't think her howling would carry that far, but she tried.

'I, Itanda . . .'

Itanda stopped her. 'It's not loud enough. Try harder!'

'*I* . . .'

'Louder.'

'*I* . . .'

'Louder.'

'I can't be any louder,' shouted Hyena. 'Do it yourself!'

A frog, who had been woken up by Hyena's howling, said the same thing. 'Why don't you just find a way to go to the Sky Kingdom yourself to deliver the letter?'

'But I can't,' said Itanda. 'I can't jump, I can't climb trees, I don't have wings . . .'

'OK,' said Frog. 'I will take it for you.'

Itanda laughed. 'What frog can do what an eagle can't do? What frog can reach where a giraffe can't?'

'I will find a way,' said Frog. 'Just give me the letter.'

'You'd better not lose it,' Itanda warned as he gave Frog the letter.

*

The next morning Frog went to the deep forest well and kept watch for the seven maidens who fetched water for the Sky Chief. When he spotted them, he wrapped the letter in his long tongue, jumped in the water and waited.

As the maidens lowered their water jugs to fill, he hid in one of them and they carried him up with them to the Sky Kingdom.

At the Sky Chief's homestead, Frog placed the letter on a small table in a corner of the banqueting room and hid in an empty water jug.

When the Sky Chief saw the letter, he read it, frowned and called the seven water maidens.

'Did you bring this letter with you?' he asked.

'No!' they said.

Since the water maidens never ever lied, the Sky Chief nodded and sent them away. He didn't tell his warrior wife or his brilliant daughter about the letter because he thought it was a bit rude really. He just threw it away.

Frog returned in the empty jug the next morning and told Itanda that he had delivered his letter, but Itanda didn't believe him.

'You mean you went to the Sky Kingdom?'

'Yes,' said Frog.

'Then where is my reply? I should beat you for lying to me!'

Frog stretched to half his full length. 'Why would you

beat the only one who can help you? You didn't ask for a reply, did you?'

'No,' said Itanda, scratching his head.

'If you want a reply, you should ask for one.'

So Itanda wrote a new letter:

> I, Itanda watcher of clouds and birds,
> keeper of the healthiest Earth herds,
> roamer of hills high and valleys wide,
> would like your daughter as my bride.
> If your response is good and swift,
> I will visit with dowry gifts.

Frog took the new letter and waited in the well the next morning, As before, the maidens took him up with them, singing their usual song as they climbed the spiderweb ladder.

> 'Up and down, such is the way of life;
> enjoy the wind whether low or high.'

When they arrived at the Sky Chief's homestead, Frog put the new letter in the same place as the first and hid close by. This time, when the Sky Chief read the letter, he called his wife and showed it to her.

'This is the second time,' he said. 'I don't know how he gets the letters here from Earth.'

The Sky Queen read the letter and bit her lip. 'He must

be very powerful. Why don't we ask him to come and meet us? Ask him to bring three gold nuggets. If he can come up here without your help then he will be worthy of meeting our daughter.'

So the Sky Chief wrote a letter to Itanda as instructed by his wife, and put it on the table where Frog had placed Itanda's letters. As soon as they left the banqueting room, Frog picked up the letter and hid in an empty water jug ready for his trip back to Earth.

Itanda was stunned when Frog gave him the Sky Chief's letter. He turned it this way and that, reading it over and over again. Although he had a reply he still could not believe that Frog had actually gone up to the heavens and returned. He read the letter one last time and turned to Frog.

'Don't worry,' said Frog. 'I will think of something. You go and get the gold nuggets.'

'But I only have cattle! How will I get my hands on gold nuggets?'

'It's simple. Exchange some cows for gold.'

'But how?'

Frog hopped on to a rock and stared at Itanda. 'Do you know how to do anything but stare?' said Itanda.

'You have to find someone who has gold first,' Frog replied.

Itanda nodded but said nothing.

'Tell me –' Frog poked Itanda – 'who has gold in the forest?'

'The dwarves do, but it's impossible to find them. And the rats too, but what would rats want with cattle?' Itanda scratched his chin.

'You should ask them. If you are not sure of anything, you should ask.'

So Itanda went off to find the rats, who kept hoards of gold nuggets in burrows, caves and hides all over the forest. He was sure they would ask him for something that he could not get in exchange for the three gold nuggets that he needed. However, when he found the chief of rats he was surprised to find that they were happy to exchange three nuggets of gold for five cows, if Itanda would teach them how to milk the cows. Fresh cow's milk was a favourite of both baby and adult rats. Itanda taught them how to clean the teats on the cows' udders and squeeze them carefully to get the milk out.

'Don't forget to milk all the udders every time,' he reminded them as he left. 'They get uncomfortable if you only milk some and leave the rest.'

Frog took the nuggets to the deep forest well in the morning and waited as he always did. When the maidens arrived, he put a nugget each in three water jugs and hid in one himself.

The maidens sang their song as they climbed back up to the Sky Kingdom.

'Up and down, such is the way of life;
enjoy the wind whether low or high.'

When they arrived at the Sky Chief's homestead, Frog jumped out of his jug and noticed that the Sky Chief and Queen were preparing a wonderful feast to welcome Itanda. Frog gathered the gold nuggets and hid as the homestead cooks carried in trays and trays of spinach and fish and cassava and beans and tomatoes and rice and spicy drinks made from ginger, hibiscus, rose flowers and dandelion leaves, as well as beers made from maize and millet.

In the evening, even though Itanda was not there, the Sky Chief's family sat around the banqueting table with all the maidens and cooks and ate a hearty meal, leaving a generous plate for Itanda – just in case he arrived later.

Frog clenched his mouth shut as he watched because he knew that his long tongue would fly out as it always did when he was hungry and smelled very good food. His belly rumbled as the cooks licked their lips and the maidens asked for more beans and the Sky Chief and Queen's brilliant daughter gobbled spinach like a rabbit. He thought she looked so beautiful – it was no wonder she was called Kamene, which meant dawn.

When they had finished eating and the Sky Chief's homestead had fallen silent again, Frog crept out and sat at the place set for Itanda. He stretched out his arms and legs, puffed his throat and belly and feasted like a chief. After he'd licked all the plates to a clean shine that glowed in the moonlight, Frog put the gold nuggets at the place where Kamene sat at dinner. Then he hopped – very slowly – back to his hiding place, for he was so so full.

He didn't go back down with the water maidens in the morning because he didn't want to return with no news for Itanda.

The Sky Chief and Queen came into the banqueting room arm in arm later in the morning to see if there might be a new note from Itanda, explaining why he had not joined them for dinner. To their surprise, the plates were bare. Not a crumb of cassava, not a shred of spinach or a drop of dandelion drink was left.

As the light is so bright in the Sky Kingdom, the gold nuggets were extra shiny where Frog had arranged them in a triangle by Kamene's dinner place. The Sky Chief gasped as he saw the nuggets and grabbed the Sky Queen's arm.

'He came,' she said.

The Sky Chief nodded. 'He must be very powerful. How did he know to place the gold at Kamene's place on the table?'

'Perhaps he's invisible,' laughed the Sky Queen. 'Maybe he's been watching us.'

'Maybe,' the Sky Chief smiled. 'But what do we do?

We can't promise our daughter to someone she has never met.'

'Well, we must make it clear to him that she'll only be his bride if she likes him, so he has to come to see her.'

'I'll write another letter,' said the Sky Chief.

By the time Frog got back to Earth the next morning, Itanda was upset. He thought Frog had tricked him and run away with his gold nuggets. He was staring at clouds, fuming, when Frog poked him with his tongue. Itanda jumped up angrily when he saw Frog.

'Where have you been? I've been waiting for two days.'

Frog held out the Sky Chief's letter. 'I didn't want to return without a response. Especially because you sent me with gold.'

When Itanda read the letter he sat on the ground and held his head. 'What do I do now?' he asked Frog. 'What do I do? I can't go up there. What do I do?'

'You have to find a way,' said Frog. 'You are very close now. Maybe one of the dwarves will have a spell you can use.'

Itanda shook his head. 'It will take too much time.'

'You just have to find them.'

'The Sky Queen wants me to come soon.' He pointed at the letter. 'There is no time.'

'Well, I can't take you,' said Frog and he hopped away, heading towards his pond deep in the forest.

'Wait,' shouted Itanda. 'Can't you help some more? Can you make them come to me?'

Frog shook his head and continued to hop home. After five hops he stopped and turned around. 'Actually, I have an idea,' he said. 'But after that it's up to you.'

'Of course,' said Itanda. 'Of course.'

When Frog reached the Sky Chief's homestead the next morning, he crept into Kamene's room and hid under the bed. When the heavens were quiet and he was sure that Kamene was asleep, he climbed out and carefully put a special glue across her eyes so she wouldn't be able to open them in the morning. The glue could only be washed away with water from Frog's pond.

In the morning, Frog returned to Earth with the water maidens and found some bushes near the deep forest well where he could wait.

Up in the Sky Kingdom, Kamene woke up to find that she was blind. She stumbled out of bed crying and tripped over the armchair where she usually read stories before she slept at night. She fell to the ground with an enormous crash and her parents rushed to the room.

'What happened?' The Sky Queen picked up her daughter and the Sky Chief checked her for bruises. They noticed her eyes were closed and asked her to open them, but she couldn't. The Sky Chief fetched some water and they washed Kamene's face, but she still could not open her eyes.

'I'm *blind*!' she wailed. 'I'm blind.'

The Sky Queen turned to her husband. 'We have to call the healers. This is not normal.'

One by one, all the famous healers in the Sky Kingdom arrived to examine and treat Kamene.

They tried rubbing herbs on her eyelids,
they tried sudden clapping to surprise her,
they tried hot water with cats' whiskers,
they tried green potions and blue ointments,
they tried chanting and drumming,
they tried cold water with owl feathers,
they tried brown oils and red powders,
they tried making her sneeze by tickling,
they tried warm water with gecko skin . . .

Nothing worked. *Nothing.*

So they all came to the same conclusion. Some very powerful creature had cast a spell on Kamene and they had to think of who it might be and settle any argument that they might have with that creature.

The Sky Chief and Sky Queen looked at each other and said, 'Itanda!'

'He's angry because we kept his gold nuggets and he hasn't met Kamene,' said the Sky Chief.

'We must send back the nuggets,' said the Sky Queen. 'We must send them and send her to be cured.'

The Sky Chief summoned the seven water maidens and instructed them to help get Kamene dressed and take her down to Earth. They were also to bag the three gold nuggets and wait at the deep forest well until a powerful man called Itanda came to heal Kamene.

So down the water maidens went, supporting Kamene (who couldn't walk straight, let alone climb down an invisible spiderweb ladder) and singing their song:

'Up and down, such is the way of life;
enjoy the wind whether low or high.'

When they got to the well, to their surprise a frog came out. He hopped right up to Kamene and put a damp cloth in her hand.

'Wipe your eyes with this,' Frog said.

As soon as Kamene wiped her eyes, she felt her lids loosen. She opened her eyes slowly to see the most brilliant green frog ever, sitting on a rock beside her. He looked like an enormous emerald with a smile. Kamene had never spoken to anyone from Earth before, so she was very excited.

'Hello, Frog!'

The seven water maidens gasped. They had seen all the

healers in heaven try to help Kamene see again, yet all it had taken was a damp cloth from a frog.

'Hello,' replied Frog with an even bigger smile. 'I will now take you to the man you are to marry.'

'I don't think so,' said Kamene. 'I get to choose who I marry.'

Frog shrugged. 'OK, Kamene; come and meet the man who sent the letters to your father to ask for your hand.'

'Wait,' said Kamene. 'How can a frog take me to the man who sent the letters? And how do you know my name?'

'Yes,' chimed in the seven water maidens. 'How?'

'Because I am a very special frog.' Frog stood to his full height on the rock. 'I took the letters to your father by riding in the water jugs that the maidens carried. I returned with the Sky Chief's replies for the man to read. I showed the man how to get gold nuggets. I delivered the gold nuggets that the Sky Queen asked for, and I sealed your eyes so that your parents would send you down to Earth. I am no ordinary frog; I can do anything I set my mind to.'

Kamene put a hand on Frog's cheek. 'Well then, you are the one that I choose to marry. I don't want to be married to a man who does nothing. I want to be married to a frog that always tries.'

And with that, the water maidens threw the gold nuggets in the bottom of the deep forest well, and they climbed up the invisible ladder with Kamene and Frog:

'Up and down, such is the way of life;
enjoy the wind whether low or high.'

Poor Itanda, the herdsman, is still waiting for a bride. He is out there staring at clouds and wondering where his gold has gone. Frog, however, was soon married to Kamene, the dawn, on a joyous, star-filled, moon-bright night in the Sky Kingdom. And every morning, just before the sun rises, you can hear frogs all over the world croaking loudly, still celebrating the biggest ever frog wedding.

A Tortoise Named Ununile

An Igbo tale

In Igboland, between the end of a year and the start of a new one, the dry Harmattan winds turn the long elephant grass in the plains brown and brittle. Snakes and giant lizards can no longer sneak up on their prey because the roots they slide between crackle like Vulture's hoarse cry. In the forest, where Mbe the tortoise lives, the mango trees carry no fruit and yam vines wither on their mounds. Even the oba trees, that stand tallest and carry fruit the longest, only have dry seedpods that fall to the ground in heaps.

Most animals in the forest stored enough food to last them until the rains came – all except the birds, who visited friends in the clouds for an annual feast. All except Mbe, the wily tortoise with the smoothest shell in the forest, who went from animal to animal begging for food until they had grown tired of him.

> He had gone to young Frog
> and both Jackal and Dog.
> He'd filched fungus from Gnat
> and begged bugs from Bushrat.
> He'd gone sideways to tap up Crab,
> climbed a tree to plead with Leopard,
> picked peels, sipped Monkey's juice
> and shared star fruit with Mongoose.
> He'd crashed the meagre feast of the ants
> and fed on the small scraps of Elephant.

There was no one else to beg from.

Mbe crawled, slow and hungry, through the forest every day, hoping to find leaves with enough sap in them to keep his stomach from rumbling.

One afternoon, he heard loud chirping and chattering near the edge of the forest, where the largest oba tree stood. Mbe went towards the noise and poked his head through wilted shrubs to see what was happening.

It was a gathering of birds of all sizes. There were big birds like Eagle and small birds like Hummingbird, there were birds with tidy feathers and birds with scraggly feathers. Mbe stretched his neck further and saw that they were crushing oba seeds and squeezing the pulp through a piece of calico cloth that Vulture was holding over a hole. They were making celebration paint!

Mbe immediately saw his chance. He was a very fine painter. In fact, he was a master in the arts of face and body painting, as he often decorated his smooth shell to help him hide from hunters. If the birds were making celebration paint, then there had to be food close by and he – Mbe – had a large and empty belly. He crawled out of hiding.

'My bird friends,' he shouted. 'Can I be of help?'

The chattering and chirping stopped and the forest fell silent. Then Pelican spoke in her strong voice. 'We know all about you, Mbe. Parrot has told us about your lazy and sly ways. We want nothing to do with you.'

When Mbe heard this he knew he could not lie, because once Parrot knew something about you he repeated it to everyone. Nobody would believe him if he said anything different.

The birds turned away from him, and continued their chirping and chattering.

'Birds, birds,' he pleaded. 'I've changed. Why, just last week, I cleared leaves from beneath this very tree and left these seedpods here for you to use.'

The birds fell silent again. It was true that there had been no leaves under the giant oba to disturb their gathering of seedpods. Of course, they had no idea that Mbe had eaten the leaves to fill his own belly.

'I see you are making paint. I would like to help.' Mbe moved closer to the circle of birds. 'My front feet are hard and wide like pestles. I can crush seeds more quickly than you.'

Apart from a few tweets, the birds remained quiet. They could see the wisdom in his suggestion; their beaks were no match for his two front feet.

Mbe hurried to finish his argument. 'Besides, I am a master in the art of uri – my paintings of faces and bodies are unmatched. I can make a stone look like a jewel, I can make a rainbow more colourful, I can give extra life to a sunset.'

Mbe moved to crouch right in the middle of the assembly of birds. Now that he had their attention, he settled into his favourite pastime – telling tales.

'You know there was a time when you birds were colourful? You didn't just have white feathers like you have now. When you took to the sky, you created patterns. My father said it was just beautiful.' Mbe paused for effect as each bird looked at its dull white feathers. As tortoises lived much longer than birds, he knew that they had no choice but to trust him.

'I can help you get those colours back. This oba you are crushing will give you yellow; I can get blue from indigo bean plants and red from dead insects. With those colours I can make all the colours in the world.'

Pigeon made a sound in his throat and faced Mbe. 'And what do you want from us? You never do anything for nothing.'

'Yes,' agreed Pelican. 'We know that you crashed the meagre feast of the ants and fed on the scraps of Elephant. And you went to Jackal and Dog and all the way to the pond, to Frog . . .'

'But I told you, I've changed,' Mbe said. 'I'm sorry that I didn't do anything for the ants or Elephant. Or that I didn't help Jackal, or Dog, or Frog. I just want to help you get your colours back because I love colours!'

The birds chattered again. They all liked the idea of having colours. Blue Jay had always wondered where her name came from; Vulture and Hawk were tired of being mistaken for each other – Pigeon and Dove too. It even happened to Swift and Swallow sometimes.

They had all heard stories about their colourful history, when Scarlet Macaw was scarlet, Yellow Warbler had yellow feathers and Rainbow Lorikeet actually looked like a rainbow. Pelican's grandfather had told her that there had been a great flood, a season of almighty rains that had washed all their colours away. And although they still painted themselves every year for the feast in the clouds, they had forgotten how to make the paint stay. It only lasted for a few days until it all faded in the sun.

Blackbird, who had always felt odd in a world of white feathers and was sometimes mistaken for Lark, stepped forward. 'Mbe,' she said, 'can you make black uri paint?'

The tortoise laughed. 'Easy, easy, easy ... Black is a mixture of all the colours, so you can't make a mistake mixing it.'

'What about green?' asked Green Hoopoe.

'Just a little blue from the indigo bean and yellow from these oba seeds and we'll have green. Easy!' said Mbe.

Pigeon flapped his wings to get everyone's attention. 'But why should we bother when the colours won't stick?' he asked. 'My grandmother said our colours were washed off by rain.'

'It's true,' said the tortoise. 'But that was an almighty rain and that only happens every hundred years or so. Everyone lost a little bit of colour then, but you birds lost all your colour, and your king, Eagle's great-grandfather, forgot how to mix colours. He also forgot the special ingredient that makes all colours stick. It comes from a plant that grows all over Igboland. You see it, girigiri like a skeleton, all over the place. It's called milk-bush.

'It's a tricky plant. When you cut it, white juice comes out. It can be poisonous, but if you use the right amount it makes colours stick. The old eagle was probably afraid to tell you because he forgot how much to use and didn't want you to get poisoned.'

The birds gasped. No one had spoken about the dead eagle king like that before. Nevertheless, before long, they had gathered round the tortoise to watch him mix colours and milk-bush juice.

Mbe painted Parrot first because he knew he was talkative and would be the most likely to tell him about the celebration the birds were getting ready for.

The tortoise was right. Parrot told him that the birds went every Harmattan to visit their winged friends in the clouds, as there was always water there. Their friends had colours, so the birds painted themselves before going so they would fit in.

'Is there food?' Mbe asked, as he put bright blue paint on the ends of Parrot's wings.

'Oh, there's a feast!' said Parrot. 'A real feast!'

Mbe felt his stomach rumble with joy. 'Oh, I would *love* to go to a feast.'

Parrot laughed. 'But you can't go. You can't fly, so you can't go. You need feathers to fly.'

'But Dragonfly and Cricket and Bat fly without feathers,' said the tortoise.

'Yes, but they are not as heavy as we are. If you are heavy, you need feathers to fly.'

Mbe looked up from the uri painting of Parrot's wings to count the birds gathered. There were hundreds. If he could get a feather from each of them, he would have hundreds of feathers. Surely then he would be able to fly too. He would be able to go to the feast.

'It's a pity that you can't fly if you lose a single feather,' Mbe said slyly to Parrot.

'What nonsense!' Parrot laughed. 'I can lose single feathers any time and still fly. Here, take this.' He plucked a newly painted red and blue feather and gave it to Mbe.

Mbe smiled and put the feather under a rock beside him.

When the birds saw the wonderful uri Mbe had done on Parrot, they all promised to give him a feather if he painted them beautifully too. So the wily tortoise set to work, designing the best uri patterns ever seen in Igboland and storing a mixed clump of feathers beneath his special rock. However, he saved his most colourful work for the birds who told him the most about the feast in the clouds, because the longer he painted them, the more they told him. If you watch birds it is still easy to tell which ones told Mbe the most. The most talkative birds in the world became the most colourful birds in the world.

> 'A touch of yellow for the beak
> and for the wings a scarlet streak.
> Orange splashed around the eyes,
> a blue crest that lights the skies,
> Uri for breast and tail and feet;
> that's how you fix a bird for a feast!'

Mbe sang loudly as he painted the birds, only stopping to ask questions. Bustard and Crane told him how *really* big birds fly. Hummingbird showed him the pattern the birds flew in on the way to the clouds. Toucan explained how the birds greeted their friends in the clouds.

By the time Mbe got to paint Eagle, who was king of the birds, but bald – like his father and grandfather – because of all the diving he did to fish, he knew more about flying and the feast in the clouds than any single bird.

Eagle was not very talkative. He stood very still and kept his beady eyes on Mbe. The tortoise wondered how such a quiet bird could be a great king.

'I have some small feathers here,' Mbe said. 'Would you like me to put some on your head?'

Eagle frowned. 'Why would I? They will only fall off again.'

'Not a chance!' exclaimed Mbe. 'Not if I stick them with my special milk-bush juice.'

Eagle thought about how his reflection would look when the rains came again and he went diving for fish. A fine crest of feathers would make him look even more like a king.

'I can just leave them white and paint the rest of your feathers in dark colours so your kingly head really stands out.' Mbe dipped his uri stick in a dark brown ink mixture.

'OK, fine,' said Eagle. 'Just make sure it is striking.'

'And can I come to the feast with you? I want to try these feathers to see if I can fly.'

Eagle laughed. 'Well, I'd love to see a tortoise fly.'

All the other birds joined in the laughter. Pigeon and Pelican were particularly loud.

'If you can fly, you can come,' said Eagle. 'We leave tomorrow at dawn.'

So as twilight broke in the shadow of the oba tree, the birds arrived to see a curious thing, a most peculiar spectacle. It was Mbe the tortoise covered in feathers of all colours. His wings were held together by milk-bush juice and were very wide – three times the length of his body. For his tail he had Pheasant's golden feather and Rooster's black feather. Mbe was a real mix of colours and patterns and shimmered in the rising sun when he moved.

'King Eagle,' he said, 'I am so grateful for this chance to fly with you and I want to repay you.'

'There is no need,' replied Eagle. 'Let's see if you can actually fly first.'

'Oh, I can fly,' said Mbe. 'I practised at night.' He lifted his wings for Eagle to see.

'Stunning!' exclaimed Eagle in surprise.

'Now,' said the tortoise, 'I noticed that you don't like to speak much, so when we get to the clouds I could make your speech for you.'

Eagle's eyes lit up. 'How nice of you to offer, but how would you know what to say?'

'I always know what to say,' said the tortoise with a wry smile, becoming his old cheeky self again. He was really looking forward to the feast.

The birds took off and flew in the shape of the letter V towards the clouds. The V worked like a pair of scissors, cutting through the air. It made it easier for the heavy birds to fly, like Pelican, Pheasant, Eagle and Mbe the tortoise, who stayed at the bottom of the V. It was beautiful teamwork and the birds, with their astounding new uri patterns and colours, looked like jewels in the sky.

Mbe was proud of his work. He floated on the warm wind, enjoying the air on his bald head. 'My bird friends,' he shouted. 'With our fantastic new patterns we should all pick party names for the feast. I choose Ununile because I have feathers from you all.'

'I choose Silverhead,' said Eagle, 'to celebrate my new crown that gleams like silver.'

One by one, all the birds picked party names to mark their uri patterns – and when they arrived in the clouds that is how they introduced themselves.

Their hosts shared kola nuts with them, as was traditional in that part of the world, and welcomed them with a song. Then their leader, a creature with scales and a crown like a cockatoo, led them to the feast and tasted every dish. Then she stood to one side. 'Now that you know that the food is safe, the feast can begin. This is for you all.'

It was the turn of the birds to respond and Mbe, the tortoise, stood up to speak on behalf of Eagle. The hosts applauded, yelling, 'King of the birds! King of the birds!'

Eagle frowned, but Mbe raised his myriad feathers to acknowledge the chants. He had planned it all. Toucan had told him the only way that the hosts knew who was the king of the birds was by his bald head. And, of course, Mbe had convinced Eagle to cover his baldness with white feathers. The tortoise was the only bald creature with feathers in the clouds – the only bald bird!

'Thank you, thank you,' he said. 'We are always glad to be in your company. You are most generous hosts and our long history of shared feasts gives us birds something to look forward to when the Harmattan winds blow and our rains begin to falter. We are always humbled by the food before us.'

Mbe paused and all the birds clapped, even Eagle, who wasn't so sure about the tortoise speaking on his behalf. It was only the beginning, but it was a better speech than Eagle had ever given.

Mbe raised his feathers and continued his speech. He retold a joke he'd heard from Peacock, remembered a story from Toucan, demonstrated a dance from Duck and ended with a song from Trogon. Then he turned to the hosts and said, 'Again, thank you. Before I finish I'd like you to repeat something for us. Who is this food for?' He pointed at the feast that was laid out in front of the birds.

'It's for you all,' the hosts shouted back.

Mbe turned to his bird companions and whispered, 'You heard their leader say that this food is for "you all" – *unu nile* – which is my party name, so I think they will bring yours out after I eat.'

The tortoise sat with his back to the birds, facing the hosts. Although the hosts thought it was odd that he was sitting alone on the other side, he was clearly the king of the birds so they said nothing.

Mbe feasted on diced bluebottles, creepy-crawly salad with almond oil, grasshopper eyes seasoned with soil, crunchy soldier ants, pickled currants, groundnuts, spiced black gnats, sun-dried maggots, tiny tiger nuts, red berries and worm bellies. He drank yellow flower juice, burped, then had some purple grape fries and steamed brains of dragonflies, termite eggs and chargrilled figs.

The birds watched in awe as Mbe gobbled the food. They thought he would stop when he had had his fill, but his belly seemed to have no bottom!

When he had eaten half of the food laid out, they started chattering.

'Look!' said Parrot. 'Mbe hasn't changed at all.'

'He's such a liar!' exclaimed Toucan. 'He tricked us all.'

'I want my feather back!' cried Hummingbird, looking at Eagle. 'Can I take my feather back?'

Eagle scratched his new white-feathered head. 'Yes, Hummingbird, what you gave freely you can always take back.'

Hummingbird hopped forward and plucked his feather from Mbe's back.

The tortoise was so busy eating that he didn't even turn round. It was as if he was in a trance – nothing could distract him.

So, one by one, the angry birds hopped to the tortoise and removed their feathers. As the food was almost finished, they took what scraps they could, thanked their hosts and began to leave.

By the time Mbe was done eating, and leaned backwards into his smooth shell, only Parrot and Eagle were still in the clouds with him. Eagle explained to their hosts that Mbe was not really their king and apologized for the tortoise's behaviour. He thanked them once more for inviting all the birds. Then he turned to kick Mbe, but the tortoise ducked into his shell.

'I'm sorry, I'm sorry,' Mbe pleaded from the safety of his shell. 'All the birds have taken their feathers back. Only you are big enough to carry me down safely.'

Eagle shook his head. 'It's too late to be sorry, because you planned this. Find your own way down.' He turned away and swooped towards Igboland.

Mbe turned to Parrot. 'Parrot, see how wonderful your feathers look. Surely you will help me?'

Parrot plucked his red and blue feather from Mbe's back. 'I'm sorry, I don't have enough feathers to help you fly. Thank you for my uri, but you will have to jump. If you can swim, I can show you the best place to jump from.'

'I can't swim!' Mbe wailed, pulling his head back into his shell. 'I'll sink like a rock. I'm trapped on these clouds!'

'So sorry, Mbe,' said Parrot. 'Would you like me to send a message to anyone if you don't make it?'

Mbe's popped his head out of his shell, his eyes bright again. 'Yes, yes! Oh, how could I be so silly? I am not trapped.' He turned to Parrot with his best smile, lowering his bald head to beg. 'Could you please ask my wife to put the mattress and all the laundry in the clearing near the palm grove? And can you whistle when she has done that?'

'No problem,' said Parrot.

'Thank you, thank you, oh, thank you!'

And off Parrot went, gliding down towards Igboland. As he flapped his wings he realized just how hungry he was. He got more and more cross with the tortoise as he got closer to home. When he got to Mbe's home, he was furious and ravenous.

Parrot knocked on the door and told Mrs Tortoise that Mbe wanted her to put all the hard things in the house in the clearing near the palm grove. He helped her build a heap of old pots and pans and wood pieces. There was even a hoe and a cutlass in the pile.

When he was done, Parrot summoned the other birds to gather in the clearing and wait for Mbe's fall, then he flew just beyond the tops of the trees and whistled for Mbe to jump.

First they heard Mbe shouting: 'I'm free. I'm a bird. I'm coming home.' But he must have noticed that the pile was glinting in the sun so he began to scream, 'No!'

His wife tried to help him by lying on the pile of hard things. He landed on top of her with a resonant bang and their smooth smooth shells broke in several places. The birds clapped and chattered, and guess what they said to Mbe?

'We know exactly what you can fix that with.'

'What?' Mbe groaned.

'Milk-bush juice!'

And that's just what Mbe did; which is why all tortoises from Igboland have shells glued together from pieces, making them a rough patchwork like a wooden quilt. Of course, they are still strong shells because they have that secret ingredient!

Marimba, the Mother of Music

An Ndebele and Zulu tale

Ngai was the god of the Masai people. Many years before this story begins, he had been wounded by Mulungu, the god of lightning, and had been driven out of the sky valley where the gods lived. After centuries of exile his wounds would not heal, so Ngai made a plan. He would capture Marimba, leader of the Wakambi people. He hoped that if he took some of her blood every day, his immortal wounds would heal.

At this time, immortals roamed and ruled the upper world, as the ancestors now rule the lower world. Immortals were born from delicate eggs of the finest coloured crystal, green as the deepest cluster of bamboo in the forest, which hummed when the night winds blew over them. Each egg hatched in just a month and out came fully formed child immortals, who grew as fast as grass does. Within two years they became adults and lived as we do, except that they all had powers beyond ours. Marimba was an immortal. She was the daughter of Odu the Ugly and Amarava the Beautiful, and was the leader and mother of the Wakambi people. She had outlived two husbands – and now her people were in grave danger.

Marimba's kingdom was weak because her son, Kahawa, had just come of age. Kahawa was a powerful warrior and was in charge of the Wakambi armies, but his inexperience and quick temper made him vulnerable. He had taken charge because Marimba was still in mourning after the death of her most recent husband.

Kahawa often went out hunting with his closest friend, Mpushu the Cunning, a large man with a rare skill for making people confide in him. One night as darkness fell they abandoned the trail of a man-killing lion and headed back towards the hilltop settlement where the Wakambi people lived.

As they spoke of past hunts and brave warriors who

had lived before them, Kahawa suddenly fell silent. He grabbed Mpushu's hand as they walked along.

'We're being followed, my friend. Don't look. Keep walking.'

Mpushu stumbled over a clump of grass. 'Is it one of the Life Eaters?' he asked.

'I can't tell, Mpushu. Just stay calm and we'll change our path. We can't let him know where our people live.'

Although Mpushu was terrified, he followed the lead of his younger companion. They took a few turns and detours through the forested land they knew so well, and doubled back on their pursuer. By the time the man – who had strange hair that sat in two bundles, one above his forehead and the other at the back of his head – noticed them, it was too late. Kahawa and Mpushu clubbed him with the jawbone of a hippopotamus and bound him securely with strips of dried kudu skin.

They bore the tall stranger on their shoulders until they reached the foot of the hill where the Wakambi lived. From there they called for the royal guards to help take the man before Marimba and her council.

Although the stranger was tied up, Marimba felt a little less safe when he regained consciousness. He stood almost a head taller than her biggest guard and he looked as determined as ever in spite of his captivity.

'Who are you?' Marimba asked in a gentle voice.

The stranger dug his toes into the ground before him, unwilling to meet her eyes.

Marimba moved a step closer to him. His hair was arranged in thick cords wrapped into bundles linked by a single cord and he wore copper earrings that stretched his ears.

'I know you are not a Life Eater; you seem to be a type of man we have never met before. Where are your people?'

The man ignored Marimba's question, grunting like a foraging hog. However, the witch Namuwiza, a senior member of Marimba's council, came forward with a sigh of realization.

'He's a scout,' she shouted. 'Why else would he be on his own so far from his land?'

Namuwiza turned to Kahawa and Marimba. 'He's clearly a scout – and that can only mean one thing. The army he was with must be only a third or a quarter of a day away. We must be on guard.'

Before Namuwiza had finished speaking, Kahawa bolted out of the room, full of the energy and rage of his youth. He commanded his town criers to grab their horn bugles and spread to all corners of the Wakambi lands. They called back everyone who was out hunting game or foraging for herbs and spices in the depths of the forest or the lovegrass-infested plains.

Before long the men and women of Wakambi were trooping into the hilltop settlement, where together they were safest. They gathered their bone-tipped spears, tightened the heads of their axes and sharpened their swords. The lookouts climbed to their posts and faded from view.

Meanwhile, Marimba's council studied the tall prisoner, noting his necklace of bones and claws, trophies of his prowess at hunting and war. His spear was longer than Wakambi spears, but the tip was made of rock and was brittle. It cracked as Mpushu squeezed it in his fist. However, his other weapon was unlike any the Wakambi had, an arch of cane tied at both ends with string and an impala skin holding a quiver of arrows.

Marimba picked up the curious weapon as Mpushu walked up to the prisoner, still holding the spear by its tip.

'You call yourself a warrior and you can't even make a proper spear!' he taunted. 'I bet you're terrified of real battle. Were you sent out to scout because you can't fight? Are you a coward?'

'Remove these cuffs and I will put you in your place. I will defeat you before you can blink,' growled the prisoner, surprising everyone by speaking the Wakambi language. 'I am Masai. We fear no one, we fear no fire, we fear no battle. I, Koma-Tembo, son of Fesi the Wolf, will not be spoken to in this manner.' He drew himself to his full height, towering over the squat Mpushu.

Mpushu stepped back, sneering. 'You say you are a great warrior, but you are our captive.'

'Not for long,' retorted Koma-Tembo. 'My father's armies are coming to destroy your people. If you set me free, I might show you some mercy.'

Mpushu wanted to strike the impudent prisoner, but Marimba put an arm on Mpushu's shoulder and addressed the prisoner.

'Why are your armies coming to attack us? We have done you no harm.'

'We are Masai,' said Koma-Tembo. 'We need no reason to fight. We conquer other people because we can. We are more than human. We are invincible and we only answer to Ngai. Where Ngai asks us to strike, we strike.'

The prisoner stamped but Marimba did not move. 'Who is Ngai?' she asked.

'How dare you question Ngai!' Koma-Tembo shouted. 'How dare you!'

He struggled to free himself from the strips binding his arms behind him, but failed.

As he fell silent, the witch Namuwiza, who had knowledge of the immortals and the gods, and could read the minds of angry men, stepped forward. 'He is speaking of the exiled god who lives in the mists of the Kilima-Njaro – Ngai of the mountains. He has taken control of the Masai and he makes them do his bidding. What I see is not good . . .' she said, as the noise made by the Wakambi returning to their huts reached the council room.

With all the Wakambi counted, the settlement's gates were closed. The warriors – men and women – were instructed by Kahawa and his deputies and took their positions for war. The atmosphere was charged with nervous energy. The elder warriors remembered the battles of their youth and itched to fight and defend their homeland again. The new warriors breathed with difficulty, their palms sweating, wondering if they would survive the coming battle and live to tell tales of it. The lookouts shivered with the leaves of the trees they hid in, silent and watchful. They saw shadows moving about three spear-throws' distance away, and turned to alert their runners to go and sound the alarm.

But, before they could pass the information on, a hypnotic sound came from the heart of the Wakambi settlement, freezing the lookouts and the assembled army as well as the advancing soldiers of the Masai.

The sound came from Marimba, who had turned Koma-Tembo's weapon of bent cane into a musical instrument by attaching a hollowed gourd to the centre of the cane. She called it a makhoyana.

By striking the string of stretched intestine, with the open part of the gourd against her bare shoulder, she made a series of heavenly notes that she arranged into a song. It was a song of love and a song of farewell:

'This land I love I won't desert.
The finest corner of the earth
where sunrise comes to wake me to
a sky that's high and clear and blue.
The brightest corner of the earth –
Wakambi girls and boys play here;
Marimba, mother of them all,
to save my home I'd gladly fall.'

The advancing Masai warriors, hearing the song and finding themselves unable to move forward, were confused. They shouted for Ngai of the mountains, their god and warrior guide, to come and save them.

'Ngai, what is that sound? What is happening to us?'

Some of them burst into tears at the beauty of Marimba's melody and tried to hide their tears by sitting on the ground and hunching forward as though they were thinking.

All the while, Marimba walked around the Wakambi settlement with her assistants, handing out to the warriors hundreds of another of her inventions. She had made it at the same time as the makhoyana. It was a sling of kudu hide, which was made to hold the kind of rough stones that could be found near the caves in the Wakambi settlement. The slings could be spun with great speed and skill and the stones released to strike advancing enemies.

As Marimba approached Kahawa's hut she stopped

playing the makhoyana, handed it to one of her assistants and went inside.

Kahawa was deep in thought and was startled by the sound of footsteps. He swivelled round, a club in his hand. He was relieved to see his mother.

'I heard the music,' Kahawa said, smiling. 'Why are you here?'

Marimba handed him three slings and showed him how to use them. When he had mastered the spinning of the weapons, she placed a hand on his arm.

'My son,' she said, 'I'm a warrior too. I have fought many battles and I can be of help against the Masai.'

'No, Mother.' Kahawa banged a fist against the wall closest to him. He felt that he was old and skilled enough to handle the coming battle by himself. Besides, his mother was in mourning and he didn't want her life endangered. He knew that, loving the Wakambi people the way she did, she would probably put herself in extreme danger just to save the people she loved.

'But, son, I am the reason they are here,' she insisted. 'I must fight.'

Kahawa frowned. 'What do you mean, you're the reason they are here?'

'Koma-Tembo, the prisoner, says that the Masai have always known about our settlement. They never bothered us before because they had enough battles to fight in Masai land and they don't like to travel far to fight. However, whatever Ngai of the mountains asks them to do, they do – and he's asked them to destroy our settlement and take me to him alive.'

Kahawa pulled a stool close and leaned on it. 'But why? I don't understand the prisoner and I don't understand their god, Ngai. Why?'

'Namuwiza says it's because of an injury Ngai got when he was driven out of the high valley of the gods. The father of light, Mulungu, shot him with an arrow that makes even immortals bleed. Over the years he has lost so much of his vitality that he now needs to drink a daily cup of the blood of an immortal, otherwise he will lose his immortality and his powers, and die. He is desperate, and I am the only immortal he can reach. It might even be wise for me to surrender to stop his vicious army from destroying our people. After all, he's only going to drink some of my blood. I won't die.'

'No, mother,' shouted Kahawa. 'You will have no freedom. You'll be like a lion or a parrot in a cage. You will not be able to roam as you love to, or make new things as you love to. It's not right for anyone to spend their lifetime serving another.'

'Then let me fight.' Marimba framed her son's face with her palms. 'Let me fight, my son. I trained you. I am one of Wakambi's best warriors.'

Kahawa didn't want his mother to fight, but he could not argue with her. She was right; she was one of the

Wakambi's best warriors. Still, he worried that Marimba would take wild risks because she was the mother of the Wakambi.

'All right, Mother,' said Kahawa. 'You can fight.'

As he spoke, his fingers tightened round the club he had been holding when Marimba came into his hut.

In a tremulous voice, she sang:

> 'Where sunrise comes to wake me to
> a sky that's high and clear and blue.
> The brightest corner of the earth . . .'

She waved at Kahawa, still singing, and turned to leave.

Marimba hadn't taken two steps when Kahawa leapt and struck her hard at the back of her head with the club. He caught her before she fell to the floor and tied her hands with one of the slings she had made for him.

He carried her to a cave in the direction where the sun set on the settlement, placed her in it and rolled a large boulder to cover the entrance. She would be safe there.

As Kahawa walked back to his hut he heard the long-awaited alarm, followed swiftly by a shower of arrows that came whistling in the wind as a band of Masai warriors advanced.

Kahawa ducked into his hut and emerged fully armed. Wakambi warriors moved into their positions across the settlement as Masai arrows struck a few Wakambi who had not retreated to their huts as ordered. The warriors in the front line spun their slings and let loose a volley of rough stones that took the Masai completely by surprise. They had no defence for slingstones flying directly at their heads as they had never encountered slings in battle before. They fell like stunned bees; many from strikes to the head, but many also from crushed knees, shattered ankles and broken fingers and wrists where they tried to protect their faces. The Masai who made it as far as the Wakambi settlement's borders fought the Wakambi front-line warriors, including Mpushu the Cunning, who battered them with spears and clubs. A few, like Mpushu, used the massive jaws of dead hippopotamuses as clubs, knocking their enemies off their feet with the back teeth of the extraordinary animals.

An angry storm brewed above the Masai and Wakambi warriors as their battle raged past midnight into the early hours of morning. As more and more fighters got hurt and fell back to treat their wounds, lightning bolts split the sky and the sound of thunder grew louder. Then a fearful bolt of lightning split a giant mopani tree in two, right in front of the two armies. It burst into flame. The fire spread fast through the lovegrass and burned the feet of the Masai, who ran screaming from the flames. Wakambi lookouts fled from their trees for fear of being struck by another bolt of lightning. By the time rain and hail followed the fierce assault of thunder and lightning, the battleground was deserted. Fear and fire had escorted the boastful Masai warriors halfway home. They had no desire to die on a rain-soaked battlefield so far from their family burial grounds.

Kahawa was in his hut with his war council – Mpushu, an old warrior called Sekuru, and Somojo the Diviner – treating the wounds he had sustained in hand-to-hand combat at the front lines.

'Did you hear that?' asked Somojo the Diviner.

'Did I hear what?' replied Kahawa. 'All I hear are the winds that come after a storm. Sekuru, Mpushu, do you hear anything?'

Both men shook their heads.

'That's exactly what I mean,' said Somojo. 'Think about it. Ngai wants to capture your mother alive and his human warriors have run away. We all know gods never give up, so what comes next?'

Kahawa nodded, slowly grasping the severity of the situation. 'He will send his super creatures, his fantastic beasts, or he might come himself.'

'Yes. So we must stay alert,' said Somojo. 'I sense the presence of night beasts.'

Kahawa immediately thought of his mother, tied up and alone in the cave. He made for the entrance of the hut just as a giant arm struck the walls of the hut down.

Kahawa looked up into the giant orange eyes of a Night Howler, a gigantic creature with talons like a vulture, green and black skin tougher than rhinoceros hide, and hoofed feet the size of a goat's. Kahawa was frozen to the spot, the Night Howler's breath making the air around him hot. Then Somojo the Diviner shouted his war name and he came to life, hurling his club directly into the Night Howler's left eye.

The eye burst with a sickening sound and leaked a foul-smelling yellow pus as the wounded creature's ear-splitting scream echoed through the night.

Three other Night Howlers appeared from nowhere, but they did not attack Kahawa and his council. Instead, they gobbled up the injured Night Howler, giving Kahawa, Sekuru, Mpushu and Somojo time to rearm themselves.

Sekuru and Somojo ran to help the warriors protecting the children, leaving Mpushu the Cunning with his friend Kahawa.

Having found the Night Howlers' weakness, they put their slings to good use, targeting the eyes of the monsters and letting their own companions eat the wounded ones.

By now, the other Wakambi warriors, with the guidance of Sekuru and Somojo, had moved all the children and the wounded warriors into caves, but the settlement's huts had almost all been destroyed by the vicious Night Howlers. All around, warriors continued to fight a seemingly endless battle. Even Kahawa and Mpushu, the two strongest warriors, were tiring.

Suddenly, they heard a deep voice behind them. 'My friends, may I fight beside you?'

It was the prisoner Koma-Tembo. His prison hut must have been broken down by the Night Howlers, but he had also been untied.

'Namuwiza,' said Koma-Tembo, as though he had read the question in their eyes. 'She freed my mind. I know of Ngai's evil now.'

With that, he took arms and all three of them fought with renewed energy until it seemed that they would soon overcome the Night Howlers.

Suddenly the temperature dropped, and an unworldly voice rang through the night.

'Put your weapons down, mortals. Ngai of the mountains speaks. When I speak I am obeyed. You are at my mercy.'

Kahawa, Mpushu and Koma-Tembo dropped their slings and turned towards the voice. A cloud of cold air hovered in the space above them. Kahawa knew what Ngai wanted before he spoke.

'Where is Marimba the immortal?'

The Night Howlers were suddenly still, awaiting instructions from Ngai. A tense silence hung over the gathered warriors where they stood beneath Ngai's cloud.

'I asked you a question, weakling,' Ngai insisted, throwing his unearthly voice directly at Kahawa's chest.

Kahawa, son of Marimba, looked above Ngai's cloud as though he could see the invisible god. 'The woman you are looking for is my mother,' he said defiantly. 'I cannot tell you where she is.'

'This is no time for sentiment, mortal fool,' bellowed Ngai. 'You have no business in the affairs of gods. I am giving you a last chance to speak, then I will have to kill you.'

Kahawa knew from the stories of Namuwiza and Somojo and his mother that the gods showed no mercy. They could be brutal to those who opposed them. His heart was beating faster than a fleeing antelope's hooves, his hands shook like a hummingbird's wings, but he could not bring himself to give up his mother.

In spite of his wounds, Kahawa rose to his full height and pushed his chest out. His love made him defiant.

'Do what you wish,' he said. 'I will not give up my mother.'

'You impudent human,' raged Ngai. 'You have twelve heartbeats to tell me or you die.'

Mpushu the Cunning wept. He and Koma-Tembo lay on the ground and begged Ngai for mercy, for more time for their friend. But the god of the Kilima-Njaro mountains ignored them.

Mpushu pleaded with his best friend to surrender, but a determined look had come into Kahawa's eyes and there was no way of changing his mind.

'Why don't you kill me now?' Kahawa taunted, throwing a stone in the direction of Ngai's cloud. 'Why should I fear a god too scared to show himself?'

With a roar of pure rage, Ngai revealed his handsome human form: a high forehead, large eyes, clear skin and the physique of a wrestler. He signalled the Night Howler closest to him, who picked up Kahawa in his enormous vulture talons, yelping with pleasure.

'Now tell me what I need to know or my beast will devour you whole.'

But Kahawa had lost his fear after his thirteenth heartbeat. He realized that Ngai could not kill him because the so-called god of the Masai needed him to tell him where his mother was. Also, if what his mother had learned from Namuwiza was true, then without his mother Ngai had very little power.

Kahawa burst out laughing, drawing shocked looks from everyone. Ngai's face turned pale and the Night Howlers shook with uncertainty.

'Do you defy me, you fool?'

Kahawa sneered. 'You can call me what you wish, but there is nothing more pathetic than a once-powerful god reduced to petty threats and thieving. You are the fallen totem of an old empire. You have made the Masai your slaves by pretending you still have your old powers, but now that you've revealed yourself I can see the weak arm you are cradling in your lap. If you had the powers of a god, you would not need me to tell you where my mother is. You are useless.'

'Silence,' roared Ngai. 'I said, where is your mother?'

'Find her yourself,' said Kahawa.

Ngai, angry now and not caring any more about his fading immortality, signalled the Night Howlers to crush and devour Kahawa.

Koma-Tembo, who had picked up the bow and arrows of a fallen Masai during Ngai's argument with Kahawa, shot an arrow right into the eye of the Night Howler holding Kahawa, and the beast dropped him.

Instantly, a horde of Night Howlers devoured the injured one and converged on Kahawa, Mpushu and Koma-Tembo. However, before they could strike, the air went still with song and they were paralysed.

The sound was the first ever produced by the instrument that Marimba would name the karimba. Made after she was released from the cave by two wounded warriors, it had a row of thin metal tines fashioned from the copper of her jewellery, attached to some wood and bent to allow them to be plucked with the thumbs. Because she carried it in a large gourd when she played, each note from the tines she plucked resonated far into the settlement and beyond, into the forest and along the silent trails of the fleeing Masai.

As the music played, the Night Howlers, enemies of all things that sound melodious and peaceful, dissolved. Their green and black rhinoceros-thick hides fell off them, leaving a mass of green with orange eyes, which turned liquid and evaporated in trails of smoke that had the foulest smell in the world.

But the power of the song was greater:

> 'Warriors at arms follow the drum;
> I move the air with just my thumb.
> Melody moves faster than spears,
> calming old wars, fire and fears.
> For all wrongs there are notes that heal;
> the sourest fruit can still be peeled.
> My weapon is song that travels
> and heals the last body that fell.
> Warriors at arms follow the drum;
> I move the air with just my thumb.'

Ngai's cloud also turned to smoke and the once imperious god of the Masai, dweller of Kilima-Njaro, Ngai of the mountains, fell to the ground like a lump of coal The evil lord of the Masai had been defeated by music.

Marimba ran to embrace her wounded son. When she released him he knelt at her feet and begged her forgiveness for striking her.

He turned to the gathered people, all the Wakambi settlement, and tattooed his palm with his dagger.

'My people, by this mark I am laying down a new law that you must obey until the end of time. No matter what the circumstances, never must any one of you strike your mother. The one who carries you for nine moons and brings you into the world is the most precious gift you have.

'By my blood, I beg forgiveness of Marimba the Beautiful – leader of the Wakambi people, daughter of Odu the Ugly and Amarava the Beautiful – who is not only my mother, but also the mother of music.'

Um Bsisi's Milk

A Berber tale

Near Zuwara, where the sun reflects like a million diamonds on the surface of the Mediterranean, there was once a fine mud nest. It belonged to a swallow called Um Bsisi who was nesting, waiting for three speckled eggs to hatch. She usually fed on moths and flying termites and dragonflies and gnats, but when the weather got particularly hot, as it was right then, she loved to have a drink.

However, although Zuwara was right beside the sea, it was also in the desert; fresh water was difficult to get and

Um Bsisi found sea water too salty, so she had developed a taste for milk. She liked Sheep's milk a little, she liked Cow's milk much more, but most of all she liked Goat's milk.

Um Bsisi was good friends with the goat. When she went flying and spotted any succulent green shoots or healthy patches of lovegrass (or even wiregrass, which wasn't as tasty as lovegrass), she would tell the goat where and the goat would go out and graze in that area. In return, Goat saved a pouch full of milk for Um Bsisi every week.

Now, because Um Bsisi was watching over her speckled eggs in her mud nest and she could not leave them to collect her pouch of milk from Goat, she asked the mouse to go and collect the milk from Goat for her. Um Bsisi begged Mouse to arrive with the milk by sunset. She pleaded because it was still the period of the fast, one day before Eid, and she wanted to break her fast with the milk. She even promised to give Mouse some of the milk when he returned with the pouch.

Mouse went on his way, walking quite briskly to make good time, but soon slowed down. He was hungry himself so he couldn't keep up his speed. Indeed, Mouse had been hoping to get some honey or milk for himself before Um Bsisi called him. Earlier, he had trekked past:

the tower that carried voices to the sky,
the seven cacti that never seemed to dry,

the six sand dunes arranged in neat rows
and the drying oasis with a single rose

to the bees to see if they had any honey to spare. But there
had been too few flowers on the trees, so there was only a
little honey for the bees.

So Mouse made his way back past:

the drying oasis with a single desert rose,
the six sand dunes arranged in neat rows,
the seven cacti that never seemed to dry
and the tower that carried voices to the sky

and went to see Sheep.

When he got there, Sheep had plenty of milk and had
set some aside, but she had just had two new babies and
was resting. Mouse didn't want to take any milk from
Sheep when she was clearly asleep. So he crept away, his
belly churning with hunger.

Mouse got hungrier and hungrier as he went past:

the farmer's homestead,
the cow,
the hyena,
the addax,
the fox,

the camel,
the brown rat

and he stopped to rest in the shadow of a cactus, then carried on past the scorpion and the jackal. He was hungrier than ever as he arrived at Goat's to collect Um Bsisi's milk.

Goat gave Mouse a large pouch of milk to take to Um Bsisi. Mouse thanked her, carried the pouch on his back and headed back, past the jackal and scorpion and brown rat ... By the time he got to the camel he was dying of thirst. He put the pouch down beside him and rested again.

Mouse hoped to get a little water from a two-headed cactus nearby, but the low part of the plant which he could reach had been drained of water. He sighed and looked at the full pouch beside him. There was so much milk in there – enough to last Um Bsisi a week or more. What harm would it do if a little mouse like him had a sip to quench his thirst? Um Bsisi probably wouldn't even notice. Besides, she had promised to give him some of the milk when he got back.

Mouse held the pouch open and had the tiniest sip of Goat's milk. It was delicious, creamy, fragrant, cool, filling and so, so, so refreshing. He couldn't help having another sip – a not so tiny sip – before he closed the pouch. He wiped his whiskers with the paw not holding the pouch and set off again, feeling full of energy and hope, going past:

the fox,
the addax,
the hyena,
the cow

and the farmer's homestead, where the ostriches were making a fuss.

In no time he had arrived at Um Bsisi's and sunset was just beginning. Mouse handed over the pouch of Goat's milk, pleased with himself for arriving at sunset. He stood by Um Bsisi's nest waiting for her to give him some of the milk as she promised, but she had a very stern look on her face, her beak clamped shut and angled downwards.

'How was the trip?' Um Bsisi asked.

'It was quite long,' said Mouse. 'I got tired and had to rest on my way back.'

'Did you get thirsty?' asked the swallow.

Mouse didn't want to admit that he got thirsty because he feared Um Bsisi would guess that he had drunk some of her milk on the way. 'I stopped by the big cactus,' he said. 'But I'm thirsty now.'

He smiled and rubbed his paws together, sure that Um Bsisi would give him some milk now. It was time to break the fast and he was sure she was thirsty herself.

Um Bsisi opened the pouch and dipped her dark beak inside. She sucked some milk and lifted her head to swallow it.

'This is excellent milk,' she said. 'It is delicious and creamy and fragrant and cool and filling . . .'

'. . . And so, so, so refreshing,' Mouse added.

Um Bsisi turned the orange part of her face to Mouse, looking at him with one eye. 'How do you know it's refreshing?'

'I'm just guessing.'

'You mean you're just guessing it's refreshing?'

'Yes, I'm guessing it's refreshing,' whispered Mouse.

'Did you drink some of my milk?' asked Um Bsisi.

Because Mouse had lied about being thirsty earlier, he felt he could not say that he had drunk some of the milk. Why would you drink someone's milk if you were not thirsty?

'No,' he said.

'Are you sure?' asked Um Bsisi.

'Yes.' Mouse nodded vigorously.

'If I find that you did, I will cut off your tail as punishment,' said Um Bsisi. 'You won't be able to wash your whole body for Eid prayers.'

Mouse was nervous but he didn't want to back down. 'I didn't drink your milk.'

Um Bsisi rose from her mud nest, exposing her three speckled eggs, and stood by Mouse. 'Then why are the whiskers on the left side of your face covered with my milk?'

Mouse lifted a paw to his face and felt the milk. Because he had been holding the pouch with one paw, he'd only been able to wipe one side of his face. He had completely forgotten. So he had gone past the jackal, the scorpion, the brown rat, the camel, the fox, the addax, the hyena, the cow and the farmer's homestead with one side of his face covered in Goat's milk.

Little wonder that the brown rat had asked him if he wanted to change his complexion.

And, of course, that's why the scorpion had said, 'You are wasting your time, Mouse; I have stung many animals and no matter what colour their fur, their blood is always red.'

Certainly, that must have been why the jackal laughed harder than ever when he went past her.

Before Mouse could think of a good excuse, Um Bsisi had cut off his tail.

'Aww!' he screamed. 'Please give it back.'

'No,' said Um Bsisi. 'You lied to me. This is punishment for your lies.'

'I'm sorry,' pleaded Mouse. 'Give me a chance to make it up to you.'

Um Bsisi returned to sit on her three speckled eggs, tucking Mouse's tail beside her. She was quiet for a long while before she spoke. 'If you replace the milk that you stole, you can have your tail back in time for Eid.'

'Thank you,' said Mouse, almost in tears. 'I will get you some milk, I promise.'

*

Although the sun was setting, Mouse set off, determined to replace Um Bsisi's milk before the next day. He really wanted to celebrate Eid with his whole body. Wincing from the pain of his absent tail, he slunk past the farmer's homestead, where the livestock were running wild because the farmer's dog had grown too old to chase them and keep them under control. Mouse jumped out of the way of two squabbling rabbits and kept going until he got to the cow's resting place, under the shade of a broken shed. He stopped to ask Cow for a bit of milk.

'Just a bit to replace what I borrowed from Um Bsisi,' he pleaded. 'Just a bit and I'll be grateful for years.'

'Well, Mouse,' said Cow, lowering her head to whisper, 'I would love to give you a bit of milk, but the bit of milk I've been saving is to give to anyone who can get me a bit of hay from the farmer. Do you think you can get me a bit of hay from the farmer?'

Because Mouse *really* wanted to celebrate Eid and he *really* needed to replace Um Bsisi's milk, he nodded, even though he wasn't *really* sure if he could get a bit of hay from the farmer. 'Yes, I think I can get a bit of hay from the farmer for you,' he said. 'Please promise to keep that bit of milk for me until I bring you a bit of hay from the farmer.'

'I promise,' said the cow with a snort.

So Mouse went back towards the farmer's homestead, where rabbits and hyraxes and ostriches were stumbling past the old dog to play in the streets and wander in the cool desert evening.

When Mouse rapped the side of a broken fence, the farmer shouted from the gate of his largest pen, 'Who is there? What do you want?'

'It's Mouse, Farmer. I've come to ask for a bit of hay to give to Cow, so she will give me a bit of milk to give to Um Bsisi, so Um Bsisi will give me my tail back.'

'Well, Mouse,' said the farmer, struggling to hold on to a turkey and a baby ostrich, 'I would love to give you a bit of hay for Cow but, as you can see, things are a bit disorganized here. I can't leave this pen to get you the hay because my dog is old and will let all my livestock wander away. And because I can't leave this pen, I can't leave the homestead to go to Mama Dog to get a new dog to help me look after my livestock. Do you think you could go to Mama Dog and get a new dog for me?'

Of course, Mouse didn't know if he could get a new dog from Mama Dog, but he knew that he had to try. Because if he got a new dog, he would get a bit of hay. And if he got a bit of hay then he would get a bit of milk. And if he got a bit of milk to replace the bit of milk he had drunk from Um Bsisi's pouch, then Um Bsisi would give him back his tail and he could celebrate Eid. So, because Mouse really wanted to celebrate Eid, he nodded.

'Yes, I think I can get a new dog from Mama Dog for you,' he said. 'Please promise to keep a bit of hay for me until I bring you a new dog from Mama Dog.'

The farmer laughed. 'I can't go anywhere without a new dog to replace my old dog, so I can't give any hay away. Of course, Mouse, I promise.'

So Mouse set off to look for Mama Dog to ask for a new dog for the farmer, so the farmer would give him a bit of hay for the cow, so Cow would give him a bit of milk for Um Bsisi, so Um Bsisi would give him back his tail, so he could celebrate Eid.

When Mouse found Mama Dog, he rushed to her side. 'Mama Dog, could you please, please, please give me a new dog to give to the farmer?'

Mama Dog turned to look at the three new dogs with her and sighed. 'I would like to give you a new dog, but I need two companions and one of these three, the sheepdog, is sick. I can't give you the sick dog because he can't help the farmer, and I can't give you one of the others because the sick one might die and I'll only have one companion.'

'What is wrong with the sick dog?' Mouse asked.

'He has sheepdog sickness,' replied Mama Dog.

'And won't he get better?'

'He may and he may not,' said Mama Dog. 'The only way to be sure is to treat him with the afterbirth of a sheep.'

'The afterbirth of a sheep?'

'Yes, the afterbirth of a sheep,' said Mama Dog. 'Do you think you could get me the afterbirth of a sheep?'

It was getting late. Stars could be seen here and there in the darkening sky. Mouse was now very tired. He *still* hadn't eaten properly and Sheep lived quite far from Mama Dog. But if he could get to Sheep and if she was awake, if he asked nicely . . .

'Mama Dog,' he said, 'if I get you the afterbirth of a sheep, will you promise to keep a new dog for me?'

'I promise,' said Mama Dog, and her companions howled as if to say yes too.

And off Mouse went, running along with no tail, all the way to the tower that carried voices to the sky and a little further to see Sheep. When he arrived, Sheep was awake and feeding her babies. She was very happy to see him.

'Hello, Mouse,' she said. 'It was very nice of you not to wake me earlier.'

Mouse was stunned. 'How did you know I was here?'

'Well, when I woke up, I saw your paw prints all over the ground with your tail mark running through them.' Sheep paused and looked behind Mouse. 'Oh dear! What happened to your tail?'

So Mouse told her everything, beginning with the tower that carried voices to the sky and finishing right back at the tower that carried voices to the sky, and, of course, the reason why he needed the afterbirth of a sheep.

'Oh dear!' exclaimed Sheep. 'You've had a very difficult day. But I'm glad that you have kept trying. And all this happened because you didn't want to wake me up earlier.'

'You looked very tired,' said Mouse.

'Bless you,' said Sheep. 'Well, you're in luck. Because I have just had babies, I have an afterbirth that you can give to Mama Dog. I also have some milk that I saved just for you!' She handed Mouse a small pouch.

Mouse took the pouch and drank. The milk was delicious, creamy, fragrant, cool, filling and so, so, so refreshing. He stared at the arrangement of stars in the dark sky as he filled his rumbling stomach, forgetting about the mild stinging pain where his tail should be.

When he finished, he thanked Sheep and set off:

to give the afterbirth to Mama Dog to get a new dog,
to give the new dog to the farmer to get a bit of hay,
to give the bit of hay to Cow to get a bit of milk,
to give Um Bsisi the bit of milk from Cow,
to replace the bit of milk he drank,
to get his tail back so he could celebrate Eid.

After all that, Mouse was rather tired and fell asleep as quickly as a star disappears in the morning, but when he woke up, he had the best Eid ever. The very best.

The Kokonsa of Asanteman

An Akan tale

Samankrom, the village where Poku the hunter lived, was close to the very centre of the forest. The trees were so high that even in the middle of the day it could turn dark, especially if the sun moved behind the canopy of the old tweneboa tree. At night, owls hooted deep in the forest. They could be heard in all the seven villages nearby, even in the largest village where the Omanhene – chief of the kingdom of Asanteman – lived. Night-time was also when the rats went to work. They tunnelled in the ground and devoured the crops that the villagers had worked hard to plant, making them disappear like magic.

Poku's wife, Yaa, was a farmer, but all her yam and groundnuts and corn had been eaten by rats, so Poku's bounty from hunting was what they both relied on for food. But Poku was down on his luck. Although he had traps all over the forest, he never found whole animals in them any more. He had caught deer, rabbits, boar, wild goats and even the most wily of forest birds – a guinea fowl – but each time he got to the traps, only the legs were left. The bodies seemed to disappear. The legs were always neatly separated from the bodies and left in a tidy pile. Everyone said it must be the work of Sasabonsam, the mysterious giant creature of the forest, but nobody had seen it.

Because there were only legs left and Poku always had to pay a tax of two hind legs to the chief of Samankrom for hunting in the forest, he only had two thin front legs to share with Yaa. In fact, when he caught the guinea fowl they had nothing to eat because a bird only has two hind legs, and wings where goats have front legs. Poku and Yaa both grew quite thin and gaunt, but there was nothing Poku could do. He kept hunting and hoping that he'd catch enough for a big meal.

One afternoon, as Poku approached a pit trap that he had set close to the river, he heard some voices pleading: 'Release us, please!'

Poku was used to odd things happening in the forest, but it was one of those dark days with no sunlight in the trees, so he took out his club and crept slowly towards the pit. He pulled back the palm fronds covering the pit and peered inside. Poku could tell that there were three creatures in the pit, but he couldn't see clearly because of the gloom in the forest.

'Who is there?' he asked.

'A rat,' said one voice.

'A snake,' said another.

'You have to save me from this rat and snake,' said the third.

'A rat, a snake and . . . what are you?' Poku cut some bushes to allow some light in and looked in the pit again.

'A man,' said the voice, just as Poku turned from cutting the bushes.

It was indeed a man. He was clearly from another village in Asanteman, as Poku did not recognize him. And beside him was a poisonous mamba snake and a large cane rat with a scar on its left ear.

Poku shook his head. 'What happened here?'

'That man,' said Rat, pointing at the tall man by Snake, 'was trying to catch me for food. I ran towards the river and fell inside this pit. He couldn't stop so he fell inside too.'

'I see. And Snake?'

'I was on that branch just above your head. That man

grabbed the branch to stop himself from falling in the pit and made me fall inside too.'

'Just get me out, please,' said the man.

'Please release us,' pleaded Rat.

Poku turned to Rat. 'You and your kind go about at night and feast on the crops that we have worked hard to cultivate. You've eaten all of my wife's crops this year. Why shouldn't I take you home and eat you for dinner?'

'I apologize for my kind,' replied Rat. 'If you let me go, I will make it up to you. I can replace . . .'

The hunter lifted Rat out of the pit before Rat finished speaking. 'Your apology is good enough for me,' he said.

'No,' said Rat. 'There is much more I can do. I can replace broken things. When you return, your wife's crops will be as they were before being eaten by my kind. And to repay you for your kindness to me, I will tell you where to find some enchanted gold.'

The rat whispered a riddle into Poku's ear before scuttling away:

> *Use Sankofa as your guide*
> *the third tallest tweneboa to find;*
> *Follow the sunset's light,*
> *go left when you think it's right;*
> *Think like a rat*
> *running from a hungry cat.*

Then Rat stopped and called back, 'Remember where my scar is. And tell no one where you find the gold or it will all disappear.'

'Thank you.' The hunter nodded and waved Rat goodbye.

Poku returned to the pit. 'Snake,' he said, 'why should I spare you? You bite my kind all the time. You even kill children.'

'I am a good snake,' said the mamba. 'I saved that rat's life by threatening to bite this cruel man if he killed him. I only bite to save lives, but if you set me free I will tell my kind to stop biting humans. Not all of them are good listeners, but I promise to tell them. Also, I will give you this very powerful snakebite antidote, just in case one of my kind bites you by mistake.'

Poku the hunter was moved by the snake's speech and lifted him out of the pit. The snake pulled a tiny pouch from under its skin and gave it to him.

As the snake slithered away, Poku helped the man climb out of the pit and then shook his hand. The man didn't say what his name was and he didn't even say thank you, which was very rude behaviour in the kingdom of Asanteman. Poku was surprised but he let the man go on his way.

So the hunter returned home, tired, hungry and with nothing except his club, his cutlass and the pouch that Snake had given him with the antidote. He was prepared to go to bed hungry, but was worried about what to tell his wife, who had grown so thin that her cheekbones were showing.

However, when he reached the footpath near their house he was surprised to hear Yaa singing and, as he got closer, he was sure he could smell yam cooking.

'Poku!' yelled his wife as soon as she heard him at the door. 'You'll never believe what happened. All my yam is back.'

She gave him a huge atuu, wrapping her arms round his neck. 'We have no meat, but we shall have mashed yam with palm oil.'

Poku was too stunned to speak, but he was happy to find that the rat had told him the truth. He put the pouch from the snake under the bed and joined his wife for dinner. While he ate the delicious mashed yam with spiced red palm oil, he thought about how he would try and solve the rat's riddle to find the enchanted gold.

Early the next morning, Poku set off for the forest. When he was halfway in, he remembered that *Sankofa* meant to go back in order to go forward, so he returned to his village and looked out across the forest skyline. He soon located the third tallest tweneboa tree. 'I think that is where Rat meant,' he said to himself, and made his way into the dark depths of the forest.

Poku dug a hole beneath the third tallest tweneboa tree, but he found nothing. He dug another just as the sun was rising – still nothing. He dug another, then another, then another . . . By mid-morning, he was exhausted. He covered all the holes that he had dug and sat down to rest, wondering how come the rat had been right about his wife's farm, but not the enchanted gold.

Before he knew it, he had fallen asleep. He woke up to the sounds of the forest: birdsong, loud cicadas and rustling in the undergrowth. He was lucky that no leopards had come his way while he slept.

It was late afternoon. Above his head, a hummingbird hovered, pecking at insects in the tree's bark; beyond his feet a lizard caught a cricket and crushed it in its mouth. Poku suddenly remembered the rest of the riddle that Rat had whispered in his ear:

> *Follow the sunset's light,*
> *go left when you think it's right;*
> *Think like a rat*
> *running from a hungry cat.*

That's what he had done wrong! He had set off too early; he needed sunset, not sunrise.

Poku waited, watching birds, snails and insects as he often did in the forest. And, sure enough, when sunset came, a tunnel of light shone directly through a gap in the bushes on to a patch to the right of the tweneboa tree. Remembering the rat's scar, he looked left instead and noticed a very thick root of the tree twisting away into a patch of shrubs, where a single yellow flower bloomed. He followed the root, and when he cleared the dead leaves and shrubs around it, found a rat hole. He didn't even have to dig! He reached into the hole and out came two large gold nuggets, gleaming even in the dim light.

The next morning, Poku went to market and bought three goats and six chickens to rear at home. When he returned, the nugget that he had taken to buy the goats and chickens was right back in the wooden box where he kept the gold. So the hunter took the nugget and went out again to buy bricks to make his house a little bigger. When he got back the nugget was in the box again, as though it had never been taken. With his own home now bigger, he decided to help his friends.

The neighbours' daughter, Aba, had been gravely ill and unable to get treatment because the healer who could help her had demanded six brown chickens as payment. Poku bought the chickens as a gift for the neighbours and went with them to see the healer. Soon Aba was cured and running home through the forest.

Poku was astounded to find the same two nuggets *still* in his box when he got home. The rat's gold was indeed enchanted.

Poku could have become rich and lazy, but he was hard-working and continued to hunt for his food. He came to be known in his village as a generous man who was always willing to help his neighbours – and anyone who was sick or poor and came to him. The goats and chickens he had bought were soon a huge family of chickens and goats, producing lots of eggs and milk and meat. Poku and his wife had two daughters, who ran faster than chickens and liked to go hunting with him on Thursdays. No rats ate the crops on his wife's farm and nobody from Samankrom had been bitten by a snake for a long, long while.

However, one day, news reached Samankrom that the Omanhene, the chief of Asanteman, had lost a case of gold. The town crier went around all the villages asking everyone to look out for the case and try to help find it. The most special piece of gold in the case was an intricate necklace that belonged to the Omanhene's trusted advisor and wife. It was made by the finest gold craftsmen in the land and was as lightweight as an evening breeze.

For days everyone seemed to be looking for the case. When Poku went into the forest with his daughters, they searched in tree trunks, by snail trails, under toad stools, in palm groves, by bamboo clusters, beside beehives and in their father's hunting traps. They found nothing – and neither did anyone else. The Omanhene desperately wanted the necklace back for his wife, so he offered a reward of five gold nuggets to find the case.

The rude man that Poku had rescued with the rat and the snake was named Koo. As soon as the reward was announced, Koo saw his chance. For years he had heard stories about how wealthy Poku the hunter had become and he was jealous. He wanted to be wealthy too. Five gold nuggets would be perfect! Two nuggets would get him a bigger house and a farm and he would still have three nuggets left to buy whatever he wanted.

Koo had already been telling people in his village that it was strange how a simple hunter from Samankrom had become so wealthy that he was known everywhere in Asanteman. Now he travelled to the palace of the Omanhene to tell him that Poku the hunter must surely be the thief that they were looking for.

By nightfall, Poku was arrested and taken before the Omanhene. He was questioned for hours, but because of the rat's warning he could not tell the Omanhene and his guards where his wealth came from. His house was searched, but no gold was found. Even the box where Poku kept his nuggets seemed empty, for the gold could only be seen when the hunter held it.

'You are a very devious thief,' the guards said. 'Where is the Omanhene's case of gold?'

'I do not have it,' replied Poku.

'So where is your wealth from?' they asked.

'I can't say,' said the hunter.

No matter how many times the guards asked him, Poku's answer was the same: 'I can't say.'

And because he said the same thing in court in front of the Omanhene's judges, he was found guilty of stealing and sentenced to execution. Koo had sworn that Poku took the case and Poku had not been able to prove otherwise. Everyone thought that he must have sold the case in another kingdom.

The day after the judgement, Poku was paraded through the villages by the executioners to teach everyone that stealing leads to death. Every lizard, bird, rat, insect, snail, snake and man saw the poor hunter being dragged along the ground in chains.

The executioners ululated, drummed and clapped. They performed spectacular acrobatics – leaping over each other, exchanging their swords in mid-air and somersaulting in groups of three and forming human pyramids. They also chanted:

> He who steals loses his tongue
> He who steals loses his lips
> Don't steal, don't steal
> Don't lose your head
> He who steals loses his head

As they approached the square where the hunter was to be executed, they began the sword dance, rotating in smaller and smaller circles until their swords just missed the hunter's body as he walked in his chains. The crowd following the prisoner and the executioners hummed a sad melody and clapped.

Suddenly, there was a disturbance from the back of the crowd. The executioners stopped dancing and a woman came running forward, crying out loud that the Omanhene's wife had just been bitten by a snake. All the chief's guards and executioners were ordered immediately to fetch the best healers to save her life.

The executioners tied Poku to a pillar in the public square and went off, leaving one guard to keep an eye on him.

The most famous healers and herb experts in Asanteman went to the Omanhene's palace to try to save his wife. But they all came out after a few minutes with her and said the same thing: the venom was too strong. They could help her live for a few more hours so the Omanhene could say goodbye to her, but she would surely die.

When the sad news reached the square, Poku overheard the guard and remembered the antidote that Snake had given him. He tapped the guard's shoulder.

'I think I might be able to help save the Omanhene's wife, but I will have to go home first.'

The guard knew that the Omanhene considered his wife irreplaceable. She was his best advisor and his most trusted confidante. The Omanhene would rather lose all his possessions than lose his wife. So the guard agreed and escorted Poku back to his house to fetch the antidote.

At the palace, Poku examined the Omanhene's wife and turned to face the Omanhene and his linguist. 'I agree with the healers, my great leader. She will not live,' he said. But all the while he was really thinking of a way to punish Koo for his false accusations.

'You are our last hope,' said the linguist. 'Something must be possible.'

The hunter nodded. 'She will not live, unless I strengthen this antidote with a special ingredient.'

'What do you need?' cried the Omanhene. 'Anything you need, you can have.'

Poku was silent for a moment, surprised that the Omanhene had addressed him directly. 'I need the skin from the forearms of a treacherous man,' he said.

'Is this a riddle?' asked the Omanhene, close to tears. 'Where will I find a treacherous man?'

The guard who had escorted Poku home stood up. He had seen how the people of the hunter's village had come out to embrace Poku because of his good deeds. As he couldn't address the Omanhene directly, he whispered to the linguist.

The linguist addressed the Omanhene. 'My chief, sometimes a lie is the truth facing the wrong direction. Your humble servant asks that you consider that the thief who stands here before you –' he pointed towards Poku, '– might be innocent and a good man.'

The Omanhene frowned for a while, then nodded slowly. 'That would make Koo, his accuser, a treacherous man.'

The chief lifted his right arm to summon his men closer. 'Guards, go and bring Koo and skin his forearms.'

With the skin from Koo's forearms, Poku applied the antidote to the snakebite and within minutes the Omanhene's wife was able to open her eyes. Attendants wiped the sweat dripping from her forehead and soon she was sitting up.

The Omanhene was so grateful that he wanted to reward Poku, but the hunter refused.

'Your wisdom has spared my life,' said the hunter. 'I need nothing more.'

'And would you like me to punish Koo?'

'It's not necessary, my chief,' said Poku. 'He has been punished enough.'

So Koo continued to live in the kingdom of Asanteman. He was still rude and still spread rumours and gossiped about other people behind their backs. Of course, his forearms healed, but they didn't return to the healthy brown colour they were before. They stayed a sickly red, and when children saw him they would chant *Hwe ni nsa kokor, nsa kokor, nsa kokor nsa kokornsa kokornsa*, which means *Look at his red hands, red hands, red hands red handsred handsred . . .* They said it so fast that it began to sound like *kokonsa, kokonsa, kokonsa* – and that's how *kokonsa* became the word for a treacherous person or a gossip in Asanteman.

The Cheetah's Whisker

A Habesha story

There once lived a girl called Abeba. She lived close to a stream called Fafen Shet, in a village that sat in beautiful savannah plains. Her home was in Ethiopia, a country full of hills and rivers and one of the first places in the world where people farmed grain.

Abeba was the happiest girl you could imagine. She spent her free time playing tegre with friends and rode her father's shoulders while shouting, 'donkey, donkey,

donkey.' When she spotted her mother, Mariam, coming home from work in the fields, she would run and skip around her, asking questions all the way home. Her father, Taddese, taught her how to write a kind of poetry called qəne, which she liked to share with her parents while they had dinner.

Every day was wonderful for Abeba, except that every now and then she yearned for a little brother or sister to play with. She sometimes wrote qəne poems about how a hand cannot make a loud sound without another hand to clap against, to remind her parents that she was lonely.

They would laugh and say: 'Be patient, child, everything happens in its time, in its own way.'

Mariam couldn't tell Abeba that she was not strong enough to have another baby. However, Abeba soon knew, for after falling sick during a season of flooding, her mother died.

Abeba became very quiet and would no longer go out to play tegre with her friends in the village any more. When she started playing again, she only played with her father. Taddese became her best friend, her teacher, her cook, her qəne reader and still, sometimes, her donkey – even though by the time she turned nine she became a little heavy for the donkey to carry.

Then one day, Taddese told Abeba that she would have a new mother, because he was marrying a new wife.

'I know you've been sad,' he said. 'I've also been sad and lonely. Gelila is a kind woman, and I'm sure you'll love her.'

Abeba made a face and said nothing.

'She has two children as well,' Taddese added. 'A six-year-old girl called Elene and an eight-year-old boy – Girma. You'll finally have playmates!'

But Abeba wasn't very happy when Gelila moved in. She had had her father to herself for more than two years, and she wasn't ready to share him. Besides, nobody could replace her mother.

Although Gelila cooked much better than her father, Abeba never ate much when she made meals and only ate properly when her father cooked. She complained that Gelila didn't make specially shaped injera for her as her mother had and put in too little salt when making doro-wat – her favourite chicken stew.

Abeba also hated her stepbrother, Girma, because he opened her notebooks and read her gone without asking and he now played tegre with all her friends in the village. She didn't like sharing a room with two other children anyway and she didn't like that Elene got to wear all the clothes that she could no longer wear because she had grown too big.

She began to wander in the hills around the village alone, thinking about ways in which life could be better. Abeba started to miss her mother all over again, even more than she had before. She wrote and sang sad songs called tizita:

> Yesterday I danced a dream
> but my arms today are broken
> only memories hold me close

She dreamed of her mother, remembering what her soft, brown skin smelt and felt like. She remembered how Mariam used to burn frankincense at the weekends, singing while washing clothes as her father looked over his students' work. How wonderful it was when she ruffled Abeba's short curly hair!

Gelila tried very hard to make Abeba feel special. She asked her what she would like to eat on Saturdays when they were all home together, she brought her little gifts from the fields, she taught her songs that she had learned while growing up, she offered to teach her how to draw portraits. No matter what she did, Abeba remained quiet and didn't respond.

As soon as the holidays came, Abeba begged her father to send her to her grandmother's. She wanted to be close to someone that reminded her of her mother, who could tell her stories about her mother's childhood – someone who would understand how sad and lonely she was.

At her grandmother's Abeba cried every day for two days. Her grandmother tried to comfort her by cooking her favourite dishes and taking her to visit cousins that she had not seen for a while, but Abeba would not cheer up. Eventually her grandmother called and asked her what was wrong.

'If you came here to be sad,' said her grandmother, 'then you had better go back home. When I see my grandchildren I want them to be happy.'

'Ayat, I'm sad and I'm lonely. My stepmother doesn't love me and now my father doesn't have time to play with me anymore. He's always with Gelila's children.'

'Abeba, your father will always have time for you. And how do you know that your stepmother doesn't love you?'

'I am not her child. I can see it in the way she talks to them. She doesn't do anything special for me; she ignores me.'

'Do you want her to love you?' asked her grandmother.

Abeba didn't know what to say, because she had never thought about it, but she wanted to feel special again so she nodded.

Her grandmother looked at her for a long time, then pulled her close to hug her. 'I think I know what is needed. This has not been done since my own grandmother was a little girl, but I think it could work for you.'

Abeba sat up, curious. 'What is it?'

'Well,' said her grandmother, smiling with her eyes just like Mariam used to, 'I can make you a love potion to give to her.'

'A love potion – that's exactly what I need,' said Abeba. She stood up and clapped. 'Yes, please.'

'Not so fast,' said her grandmother. 'It's a very complicated potion to make, but I can do it. It's just that there is one ingredient that you would have to get for me.'

'Anything, Ayat, I'm ready.'

'OK. The thing that I need to finish off the potion is the whisker of a cheetah.'

Abeba's jaw dropped. There was no one in the world more scared of cheetahs than Abeba. 'A cheetah's whisker?'

'Yes,' smiled her grandmother. 'Do you think you can get one?'

'Of course,' nodded Abeba, not wanting to give up. 'I'll go out tomorrow and start searching.'

Abeba knew that the cheetahs of the savannah slept for hours every day in shaded areas of high grass. When Abeba had gone to the edge of her grandmother's village to fetch water, she had never travelled much further – except in the direction of her own village. In every other direction, the isolated clumps of thorn trees looked scary. However, she set off the next day on her quest, knowing that she would have to go beyond all the paths she had known before, leaving behind the comfort of knowing where she belonged.

There weren't many places to hide in the open savannah. The hollows of abandoned anthills provided shelter here and there and sometimes there were caves. However, other animals lived in most of the caves and it was dangerous to intrude.

But Abeba was determined to have the love potion, so she carried on. Past the dark red sands that marked the edge of the village, past the stubborn clumps of low elephant grass that seemed to survive regardless of the weather, beyond the patchwork scatterings of spear grass and into higher clusters of mixed beard grass and lovegrass.

The grass was as high as her waist and made a pleasing, swishing sound as she walked through it. After a while she heard the distant trickle of a stream, so she climbed a nearby tree to look for it. She couldn't see the water itself, but Abeba could tell from the richer green of the grass towards the east, where she had to shade her eyes from the early sun, that it was there.

As she prepared to get down from the tree she saw a movement in the grass close to the stream and waited. She held her breath, her heart beating faster and faster, until she saw the creature through the grass; its thick tail, its distinctive markings, its smooth gait. It was a cheetah, a lone cat. She watched it move away from the stream and stop under a cloud-shaped bush. It stretched backwards then lay down to sleep.

Abeba got down from her tree and walked towards the cheetah. When she was close enough to hear the low rumble of the cheetah's breathing, she found another tree and crept even closer to rest beneath it and watch the sleeping animal.

Although she was scared, she felt close to the cheetah because, like her, it was alone. She was fascinated by the contrast between its white belly and the rest of its coat, like a secret it carried.

Abeba watched the cheetah all day until it woke again. It sniffed the air as though it sensed her presence. Its whiskers twitched and it let out a low growl as it yawned, tossing its head before it ambled back towards the stream. Abeba returned to her grandmother's, determined to return the next day and get closer to the cheetah.

While helping her grandmother cook the spicy beef key-wat stew that evening, she thought about the cheetah's black tear marks that ran all the way down to the sides of its mouth, making it look sad and funny at the same time. Abeba hummed a tizita, but with a smile on her face.

> Yesterday I danced a dream
> and if today my arms are gone
> can my feet find a new rhythm?

She saved a large piece of raw meat from the key-wat to take with her the next day.

Abeba was up and by the cheetah's bush just after sunrise. The light threw her shadow behind her as she crept back to the tree she had found the day before to watch the cheetah.

The cat surveyed the horizon, now and then pausing to sniff the air. Abeba was as still as an anthill and breathed slowly through her mouth into her hands. She felt sure that the cheetah sensed her presence and it seemed to pause before settling down to sleep. When she was certain that it was in a deep sleep, Abeba left her hiding place and tossed the meat from the night before close to the sleeping animal.

When the cheetah woke up, it caught scent of the meat and slunk towards it. It sniffed the meat cautiously, then lifted it into its mouth in one swift movement. As it chewed it sniffed the air, as if sensing Abeba's presence again, then made a soft growling noise before returning to rest under its bush.

Abeba watched the cheetah as she did the day before. She realized that she now found the sounds that the cheetah made familiar. She could tell when a growl was contented, when one indicated hunger or thirst. She could guess from a tone of purring that the big cat was about to sleep. She waited until the cheetah went towards the stream to drink and crept away for the day.

She returned the next day with more raw meat. This time Abeba did not wait for the cheetah to fall asleep. She stood up and tossed the meat towards the beast then walked slowly to her hiding place. She watched as the cheetah gobbled the meat and observed, stunned, as it seemed to toss its head in her direction. She thought that perhaps that was its way of saying thank you. Yes, she said to herself, yes.

Abeba headed back to her grandmother's with a skip in her step. She zoomed past the high clusters of mixed beard grass and lovegrass, the patchwork scatterings of spear grass, the stubborn clumps of low elephant grass and the dark red sands that marked the beginning of the village, to help her grandmother chop up ingredients for key-wat.

With the onion cooking in the niter kibbeh oil and her grandmother grinding more spices to add, Abeba crushed garlic cloves and paused to ask about the love potion.

'Ayat, when you get the whisker, do you chop it or grind it, or do you just boil it for flavour like you do with bones for soup?'

Her grandmother brushed a handful of spices into the pan over the nicely-browned onions and looked at Abeba, a twinkle in her eyes. 'Just get it first,' she said. 'Get it and I'll show you.'

'OK.' Abeba took a piece of meat and wrapped it in leaves for the next morning.

At the cheetah's resting bush, the next morning, Abeba did not retreat to her hiding place after she tossed food to the cheetah. She crouched close by and watched it eat. She remained in the same position as the beast stared at her. It purred and sniffed the air in her direction, as if making sure that it was a scent it recognized, then turned to look across the wide expanse of the savannah. After a while, the cheetah growled softly and rose to go towards the stream.

Abeba returned daily with meat, moving closer to the cheetah each time.

One morning, after a few weeks of her visits, she was surprised to find the cheetah gone when she arrived. She thought that it might have walked to the stream early, but after a couple of minutes she heard a growl behind her. Abeba realized that she was surprised but not scared. She tossed the meat she had brought to the usual spot and the cheetah slunk past her, brushing its thick tail against her arm as it went to eat.

Feeling bold after her encounter, Abeba went to the cloud-shaped tree a little earlier the next morning to spring her own surprise on the cheetah. She crept up behind the big cat and stroked it along the thick patterned fur on its side. The cheetah purred, raised a large front paw in the air for a second and growled.

Abeba placed the piece of meat she had brought in front of the cheetah. As it ate, she reached out and pulled a whisker from its face, tucking it into a little fabric pouch that her mother had made for her when she was younger. She stayed beside the cheetah as it stared across the horizon and stood up with it when it rose to head to the stream for a drink.

Abeba went in the opposite direction, a bit sad to be leaving her new friend, but broke into an excited run as she approached her grandmother's home.

'I have it! I have it!' she screamed as she burst into the kitchen. 'I have the cheetah's whisker. Now we can make the potion.'

Her grandmother laughed and gave Abeba a big hug.

'Come and sit down, my child,' she said, leading Abeba to her bedroom.

'Now, tell me, how did you manage to get a whisker from a cheetah without getting any bites or scratches?'

Abeba sighed. 'I took my time. I watched it and tried to understand its habits. I knew that it had to trust me and I needed to lose my fear of cheetahs, so I was patient. I took it something to eat every day and got closer each time. After a while, I could tell that it expected me and waited for me. When I felt like it trusted me completely, when I felt that I could call it my friend, I sat beside it while it ate and pulled out a whisker.'

'That must have been very difficult for a girl like you; you're intelligent, but very, very, impatient,' said her grandmother with a knowing smile.

'Well,' said Abeba, 'I knew the whisker was important to you, to help make the love potion. Can we make it now?'

Abeba's grandmother looked her right in the eyes, holding the girl's face between her small, dark hands.

'Abeba, you don't need a potion. You were patient with a cheetah because you knew it was important to me. Now try being patient and attentive with Gelila and Elene and Girma because it's important to your father. You'll see it's a lot easier than making a love potion.'

Abeba nodded, tears welling in her eyes.

Her grandmother wiped her tears. 'And remember that I don't like to see you unhappy. It's important to me and your mother that you smile every day.'

Where the King Washes

A Mauritian tale

On the east side of our island, where petrels swoop down at dusk to fish, where bats unfold their wings to float and catch insects in the cool night air, there is a family of hares who avoid going anywhere that tortoises can be found. The reason for that is a story that the birds still tell. Indeed, even the bats, blind as they are, tell it well.

There was a king who lived in the castle up on the first hill from the eastern coast, not far from Trou d'Eaù Douce. Like all queens and kings before him, King Samir was kind, had a melodious laugh, smooth, smooth skin from his daily scrub, loved all sorts of curry dishes – especially hot curry dishes that he invented himself – and did not like wearing his crown. But King Samir was a little odd too. Not odd-looking, but odd like a chicken that doesn't like to eat corn or worms; King Samir absolutely, positively hated having his bath in the castle.

There were eleven bath pools in the castle; two in the grand huts beside it, where his guards lived; one by the gate to the castle; and two by the farm, for the families that looked after his donkey, six horses and livestock. But somehow King Samir preferred to bathe in a large pond that was down the hill from the castle, surrounded by high takamaka and manglier trees. He loved the pond so much that he had forbidden anyone else to bathe in it.

He called his favourite guard, Vikas – son of the old king's guard – who had been his friend since he was seven years old. He put on his shorts, picked up his towel and walked down the hill, whistling a song he'd learned from his father as he did so:

> Down the hill and down below,
> down into the magic pond.
> When I feel a little hot,
> that's where I like to go.

When he got there, he hung his things on a low branch, dived into the clear water, swam underwater to the opposite bank, then on his back to the middle of the pond. Wading in the middle he let the sun play on his dark skin for a while, then he returned to the bank to wash himself properly.

He had been doing that every day since he was young – ever since his father first took him as a nine-year-old and he fell in love with the place. And he kept doing it every day until one day he got to the pond and found that it was dirty. It was so dirty that it looked like a mud bath.

King Samir was furious. 'What's happened here?' he asked Vikas, although the guard had arrived *after* him, carrying his towel and change of clothes.

Vikas, who was half a head taller than the king, shrugged just as a drop of water from a takamaka tree fell on his nose. He remembered that it had rained the night before.

'I think it rained, my chief,' he said. 'That might be why.'

King Samir laughed one of his loud, melodious laughs. 'Ah, yes, you're right. Let's go back then. We can return tomorrow.'

And off they went, back to the castle, where King Samir had a lunch of milkfish and gecko curry, one of his invented dishes.

The next day he went back down to the pond, whistling the same song as always, very excited that he would finally have his bath.

> . . . down into the magic pond.
> When I feel a little hot . . .

Before they had gone past the high manglier and takamaka trees that surrounded the pond, King Samir tossed his towel to Vikas and ran towards the pond. He almost, *almost* jumped in, but he stopped at the edge. Only one toe – the big one on his left foot – got wet. The pond was dirty again.

When Vikas arrived, he was surprised to see the king sitting naked beneath a tree. He picked up King Samir's shorts and passed them to him.

'Did it rain again?' asked the king.

Vikas looked at the ground. It was drier than the tip of a rhinoceros' horn. 'No, my chief,' he said, shaking his head.

'Then you must stay here and find out what's happening to my pond,' said King Samir.

'Right now?' asked Vikas, hoping he would be able to go to the castle to get some food before keeping watch as he was already quite hungry.

'Yes. I need you to watch this place every minute until I come back tomorrow.'

King Samir stamped his feet as he walked away from the pond, but soon he could be heard whistling as he climbed the hill towards the castle.

Vikas settled on the ground between two wide-armed frangipani trees and fixed his eyes on the pond. As the sun rose, the shade from the trees kept him cool and he shaded his eyes at midday when the sun reflected off the pond into his eyes. He sat like that for many hours and nothing happened . . .

Actually, he noticed, something *had* happened. He stood up and walked to the edge of the pond. It was clear! Just the way King Samir liked it.

Vikas smiled. The king would be happy tomorrow.

But Vikas's smile couldn't fight his hunger. His stomach really started to rumble and he wondered if it was worth staying by the pond right through the night, as it was so, so, so deserted. He leaned back against one of the frangipani trees and closed his eyes – just for a second, he thought. Just for a second.

There was soon a rustle in the undergrowth, the lovegrass at the edge of the trees moved this way and that. Vikas didn't hear a thing. He was sound asleep.

The grass separated and a face peered out. It was the hare. He noticed Vikas sleeping beneath the frangipani and crept close to him to check if the guard was really, really fast asleep. He tore a stalk of grass and tickled Vikas's nose. The guard grunted but he did not wake up.

The hare took six quick leaps and dived into the warm, clear water of the pond. He did:

the backstroke,
the front crawl,
the hare flick,
the butterfly
and the breaststroke.

He scrubbed beneath his armpits and under his strong hind legs, then he swam to the far bank of the pond and took out a long pole that he had concealed there.

Hare pushed the pole into the water and used it to stir mud from the bottom of the pond until the pond's surface was very, very muddy. He put the pole back and was drying himself in the setting sun when Vikas woke up.

'Hey,' Vikas shouted when he saw the hare. 'What are you doing here?'

Hare, a very cheeky fellow, shouted back, 'What does it look like I'm doing here?'

'It looks like you're lying in the sun,' said Vikas, frowning and getting to his feet as his eyes adjusted to the new light.

'Well then, that's what I'm doing,' said Hare. 'I'm lying under the sun.'

Vikas ran to the edge of the pond, surprised to find it muddy again – far more muddy than before.

'What happened here?' he asked Hare.

'What do you mean, my friend?' said Hare. 'I'm just lying under the sun. I saw nothing happening here, but you were asleep when I came.'

Vikas put a hand to his forehead, wondering what he would tell King Samir. 'Was the water muddy when you came?' he asked.

'The water's always muddy when I'm here,' said Hare, picking up his belongings to leave.

So Vikas was left by himself watching the water all through the evening, his stomach rumbling with no food. At night, the moon came to sit like a fat, white hog in the middle of the pond, making the surface look clear when the water wasn't. Bats came swooping over the surface to catch flying insects and at dawn a chorus of different birds:

kestrels,
doves,
fighting terns,
parakeets,
warblers,
impatient quails,
herons,
pigeons
and one albatross

gathered at the edge of the pond to drink water.

> Down the hill and down below,
> down into the magic pond.
> When I feel a little hot
> that's where I like to go.

King Samir arrived with another guard, one of the new ones, carrying food for Vikas, who was so hungry that he started eating mangoes before he told the king what had happened.

The king flung his towel on to a low branch and rushed to the pond. He almost, *almost* jumped in the pond, but he noticed that it was muddy and stopped at the edge. Only one toe – the big one on his left foot – got wet.

'*Vikas!*' he shouted. 'Why is my pond still muddy? What happened?'

'My chief, I watched the pool right through the day like you asked. It became clear in the afternoon, but . . .' Vikas looked at the ground and scratched his right ear.

'But what?' asked King Samir.

'My chief, I was very hungry. I . . . I fell asleep for a couple of minutes. When I woke up, the hare said nothing had happened.'

'The hare? A hare? A *hare*? You were talking to a hare instead of watching my pond?'

'No, my chief, the hare was sunbathing and he said . . .'

'A sunbathing hare?'

'Yes, my chief.'

'I don't want to know what a sunbathing hare said. Do you know what happened to my pond?'

'No.'

'Then go away. Back to the castle. You are not my favourite guard any more.'

'You –' King Samir turned to the new guard – 'you can have all this food. It is enough to last you until morning. I want you to watch this pond and let me know what happens to make it muddy.'

As Vikas had the day before, the new guard settled to watch the pond. Because this guard had lots of food, the time seemed to pass more quickly for him. He wasn't grateful for the shade of the frangipani, he didn't notice the sun reflecting off the clear pond at midday and his stomach certainly didn't rumble.

But there was soon a rustle in the undergrowth that made him sit up. The lovegrass at the edge of the trees moved this way and that.

The grass separated and Hare peered out.

'My good man,' said Hare, 'how are you today?'

'I'm fine,' said the new guard, still surprised at the hare's sudden appearance and his confidence.

Hare, on the other hand, had come prepared after the surprise of the day before. He produced a gourd from behind him.

'I can see you've got some lovely food there, but this . . .' Hare tapped the side of the gourd. 'This is honey from the Ilomiel region, where my parents live. You simply *have* to taste it. There is no better anywhere in the entire world.'

The guard frowned, but he stuck his finger in the gourd and put some honey on his tongue.

The hare jumped up and down. 'Tell me! Tell me! Tell me! Tell me!'

'It's good,' the guard nodded, taking another scoop of honey, then another. Somehow he couldn't stop himself.

'Here,' said Hare, holding out the honey. 'Drink it straight from the gourd.'

Well, none of the eighteen rivers of Mauritius – big or small – could tell you what was in that honey, but the new guard was asleep and snoring before he had had half of the honey in the gourd.

Hare sat on the sleeping guard's stomach, picked up a plate and feasted on the food that King Samir had left for the guard to eat. When he finished, the hare took six quick leaps and dived into the warm, clear water. He did:

the backstroke,
the front crawl,

the hare flick,
the butterfly . . .

He scrubbed beneath his armpits while doing the breaststroke and sang at the top of his voice:

> 'Good for the King and good for the hare,
> fro-lic-King in some cool valley air;
> I swim and scrub and float and glide-ee
> in the fading glow of sunshine-ee
> ee ee ee ee ee ee ee ee
> what a joyful fee-ee-ling!'

Hare's singing didn't wake the new guard up. He didn't see Hare take out the pole and stir the water in the pond to make it muddy. He didn't see Hare sunbathing or notice the moon sitting in the middle of the pond, making it look like that water was clean.

He was fast *asleep*. He didn't see the coming of dawn or the chorus of different birds:

kestrels,
doves,
fighting terns,
parakeets,
warblers,
impatient quails,

herons,
pigeons
and one albatross

that gathered at the edge of the pond and lifted their curved beaks towards the sky as they drank water.

He only woke up when King Samir picked up the hare's pole and poked him with it.

'Hey,' said the king. 'What happened here? Why is my pond still muddy? Why were you asleep?'

The guard rubbed a hand across his face and looked around. All the food was gone. He remembered the honey, but he couldn't find the gourd. He blinked at King Samir and Vikas, who were watching him expectantly.

'The honey,' he said.

'What honey?' asked King Samir. 'I'm asking you what happened here. Why is my pond still muddy?'

'I don't know,' said the guard. 'A hare offered me some very sweet honey, but I don't . . .'

'*A hare? A hare?*' King Samir was furious. 'Get out of here. You're fired! You'll never work again on this island.'

News quickly spread about King Samir's rage and his offer to pay eight pieces of gold and a bag of rice a month to anyone who could solve the mystery of his muddy pond. The king had started to stink a little because he hadn't washed in five days. However, nobody went to apply for the job because King Samir had declared that anyone who got the job and failed would have their head cut off.

On the eleventh day of not washing, when the king had locked himself in a private room to avoid the flies that followed him everywhere, there was a knock on the door.

It was Vikas, who was still his favourite guard. 'My chief, I have a tortoise here to see you about the pond guard's job.'

King Samir doubled over, laughing his loud, melodious laugh. 'Vikas, first you tell me about a hare – a sunbathing hare – now you're bringing a tortoise guard? Is this a joke?'

'No, my chief, I'm serious. She's right here.'

King Samir peered round the door and saw a large tortoise to the left of Vikas. The top of her shell was almost as high as the guard's knee.

'Why, hello!' said the king. 'So you want the job?'

'Yes,' said Tortoise.

'And you know that if you fail you will lose your head, right? I've never had tortoise curry before.'

'I've never failed before,' said Tortoise, stretching her neck out of her shell. 'This neck of mine will never be scarred. I will solve your problem in a day.'

And off she went!

*

First Tortoise got her shell coated in the finest black
then she went to the pond and sat exactly where the guards
sat under the frangipani. *Except* . . .

she pulled her legs into her shell
she pulled her tiny tail into her shell
she pulled her cunning head into her shell

She looked like a rock.

Sure enough, just as the sun was moving from its highest,
hottest position in the sky, there was a rustle in the
undergrowth, the lovegrass at the edge of the trees moved
this way and that, the grass separated and Hare peered
out.

He was surprised to see a rock where the guard should
have been, and was very suspicious. He walked around
the rock and poked it. He tickled it with a stalk of lovegrass,
he tried to surprise the rock by shouting, he watched it
very closely to see if it would move.

Nothing happened.

'Well,' said Hare to himself, 'the king's given up and
had a rock put here for me to relax on. I will have a great
time today and that calls for a song!

'Good for the King and good for the hare,
fro-lic-King in some cool valley air;

I swim and scrub and float and glide-ee
in the fading glow of sunshine-ee
ee ee ee ee ee ee ee ee
what a joyful fee-ee-ling!'

Hare decided to do his six leaps to the pond from the top of the rock, the way he had done from the new guard's belly.

He jumped on to the rock, but . . .

He *couldn't jump*. His jumping foot was stuck! The tar on Tortoise's back had gripped it fast.

Tortoise popped her head out. 'I hope you're comfortable,' she said. 'I'm taking you to the king now.'

Hare was very surprised and very angry. 'Hey, no! No, you rascal. Let me go or I'll have to beat you up. I don't like to hit a lady, but I will!'

Tortoise popped out her legs and tail and laughed. 'You can try.'

'I'm not kidding,' said Hare. 'People think all my strength is in my jumping leg, but the other legs are just as strong. Take this!' He struck the tortoise's shell with his other hind leg and . . .

It got *stuck too*!

'OK, Tortoise,' he said. 'Enough kidding now. If I have to use my front legs, you'll be sorry. I throw better punches than any boxer.'

He lifted one paw high and struck. 'Take this round-house punch.'

The paw got stuck.

Hare was so annoyed that he struck again with the other paw. 'And take this.'

Now all Hare's limbs were stuck and Tortoise was halfway up the hill to the king's castle.

'Tortoise,' warned Hare, 'let me go now or I'll have to hurt you.'

'You can't hurt me,' said Tortoise. 'I'm in my shell and I can't feel any of your blows. I'm in a very safe space.'

'Oh,' boasted Hare in spite of his situation, 'you haven't heard about the power of my head, have you?'

'Show me,' said Tortoise, laughing.

And, of course, Hare did. So he arrived at the castle unable to move any part of his body.

The cook released Hare from Tortoise's shell with hot water and tied him up next to the hot coals, ready to make curry with his flesh.

Tortoise told King Samir how she had caught Hare and the song he sang before he got stuck:

> 'Good for the King and good for the hare,
> fro-lic-King in some cool valley air;
> I swim and scrub and float and glide-ee
> in the fading glow of sunshine-ee
> ee ee ee ee ee ee ee ee
> what a joyful fee-ee-ling!'

The king found the story and the song hilarious. He thought it wouldn't be so bad if other people used the pond as he only used it in the mornings. He laughed his loud, melodious laugh and commanded that Hare be pardoned. He also asked Vikas to announce that the pond could be used in the afternoons by anyone on the island.

Hare ran straight back to the woods, but there still remains a black patch behind his neck from being so close to the cook's hot coals.

As for Tortoise, she walks even more slowly now, weighed down by all the gold from King Samir.

PUFFIN CLASSICS

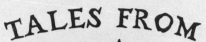

TALES FROM

AFRICA

With Puffin Classics, the adventure isn't
over when you reach the final page.
Want to discover more about the people
and places that inspired these stories?
Read on . . .

CONTENTS

Africa is amazing! It's the second biggest continent, with the second biggest population, in the world. It also has the longest river – the River Nile flows for over 6,400 kilometres. It has the biggest desert – the Sahara is almost as large as the United States of America, and has sand dunes that are over 180 metres high. People from the continent speak thousands of languages and almost every person speaks at least two languages. Scholars think the first human beings came from Africa, and Egypt is the oldest civilization in the world.

The equator runs through the middle of Africa, and it is the only continent to stretch from the northern temperate zone of the world to the southern temperate zone. This means that it has an enormous variety of climates and habitats, from equatorial rainforests to subarctic conditions on some of its mountain peaks. It is the hottest continent on earth.

Africa is home to thousands of species of animal. Lions and cheetahs are among the hunters of the grasslands, where there are huge herds of antelopes and gnus. Giraffes and zebras also live there, as do herds of elephants and rhinos. Hippos and crocodiles are found in tropical rivers, lakes and swamps, and monkeys, chimpanzees and gorillas live in the forests. You can also see flamingos and ostriches – and there are even penguins in South Africa! Unfortunately trophy hunting and destruction of habitats by migrant European farmers and tourists have reduced the numbers of species you can see nowadays.

There are also many different trees, including various palm trees. Along the Mediterranean coast you find olive trees, cedars and cork oaks, and papyrus reeds grow along the River Nile. The rainforests of west and central Africa have hundreds of different trees, including mahogany, kola, ebony and iroko. The fruits of the ebony are known as jackalberries. The tweneboa is a softwood, used to make furniture, musical instruments and other items. Large scale harvesting for use in commercial furniture manufacturing in the USA and Europe has led to a huge reduction in the number of tweneboa trees. It's now on a list of threatened species, but countries like Ghana are planting new tweneboa forests – although it can take over ten years for a tree to be fully grown! In most of Africa – especially eastern and southern Africa – there are euphorbia bushes, which are also called milk-bushes because of the white sap that appears when they are cut. There are also myrrh trees, and plants such as giant groundsels and lobelias. The great grasslands contain trees that are resistant to drought and fire, including baobab and acacia trees. Elephant grass grows in tall clumps like bamboo. It attracts moths that can damage maize crops, so farmers plant it near their fields to protect the maize. But, as with animals, commercial farming has destroyed many native African plants. Forests were cleared for farming, and hunters started fires to drive game out of grasslands. Overgrazing means that some grasslands have turned into deserts. Efforts are now being made to reverse some of these problems, but it is a long and difficult task.

PEOPLE AND LANGUAGE

There are over 800 different ethnic groups in Africa, and more than 1,250 languages (some scholars believe there are over 3,000 different ones!). The continent contains 54 independent countries, as well as other territories, each one with a huge mixture of people and languages – for example, about 80 languages are used in Ethiopia, and around 500 in Nigeria! Some of them are sign languages, or ones used by only small groups of people; many of these languages have little in common with any of the others.

Most African people speak more than one language, with Amharic, Swahili and Hausa being used very widely.

Over centuries, many people from other parts of the world have come to Africa – to trade, to live, or to exploit. As a result of this, Arabic, Dutch, English, French, German, Italian, Portuguese and Spanish – or versions of these languages mixed with local words – are all found here; people from India and China have also settled in Africa. However, even if you took away all the languages from outside the continent, there would still be hundreds left. And each language reflects the lives and customs of the people who use it – words for hunting, perhaps, or weather, or music and dancing.

How many languages do you know? Maybe you and your family speak or read other languages than English. How many people in your school speak other languages? Make a list of all the ones you can think of, or the ones spoken by people you know. Can you find out how to say 'Hello', or 'Good morning' in all of them?

CRAZY CREATURES

In Madagascar, we are told in the stories, there was a time when animals and birds could be mixed up: 'You could be a crocodile and a grasshopper – a crochopper, or a snail with the red blood of a lion – a snaion.'

There are animal crosses in the world today – a mule is half donkey, half horse, a liger is half lion, half tiger, and there are dogs that are actually half wolf (and wolves that are half dog).

However, the mothers and fathers of these animals are closely related, and their children look like one or other of their parents. What would happen if we could do what the storytellers of Madagascar described, and put halves of completely different animals together? Would a combination of a sheep and a goldfish be very good at swimming and have a woolly orange coat? Would it be a sheefish or a goldeep? Would a half-cat, half-pigeon be a cat able to fly home over long distances, or would it be a bird that caught mice?

What is the strangest combination you can think of? Draw a picture of your new creature, name it and describe what it might be able to do.

HOW WOULD YOU PAINT YOURSELF?

Mbe the tortoise (in the story 'A Tortoise Named Ununile') paints all the birds in glorious colours to go to a party. In his part of Africa this skill was called uri. Of course, Mbe is doing it for selfish and greedy reasons, not because he wants the birds to look lovely.

These days, birds don't paint themselves, but people do! It's something we've done for many centuries. In Iron Age Britain men used woad to paint themselves with all sorts of blue patterns when they went into battle. The Maori of New Zealand also painted themselves when going to war – it helped frighten their enemies. Modern soldiers colour their faces and hands with green, brown and black paint as camouflage if they think their skin will show up in action – and in some South American countries soldiers on parade colour their faces so that people can see which of the many native peoples they belong to.

Battles aren't the only reason for painting your body. People in many countries wear nail varnish. Actors may paint both their faces and bodies to change the way they really look. Maori and other Polynesian peoples, aboriginal Australians and various groups of people in Africa all paint themselves for religious and other ceremonies. The patterns may also show which clan or family group a person is from.

The paints are often natural pigments – coloured earths that will come off easily. When plants like woad are used, they stain the skin and it takes longer for the patterns to fade. In South America juice obtained from the bush now called huito (*Genipa Americana*) was used for a dark blue or black dye: originally worn in battle, it's now used for jagua tattoos – very fashionable decorations that last for about a fortnight!

In India and some North African countries skin dyes have long been used for adornment – girls and women, especially brides, use the reddish-brown dye from henna leaves to paint wonderful patterns on their hands. Sometimes the spice turmeric is also used to give a yellow colour. Anyone who uses modern cosmetics such as lipstick or eyeshadow is following in the same tradition – using body paints to look more beautiful!

There are other reasons to use paints on your face or body: circus clowns paint their faces – every clown has his or her special design which no other clown is allowed to use. And many people will have seen 'living sculptures' – mime artists completely covered in white or silver or gold paint, standing as still as a statue – but if you throw coins into their collecting plate, they will move very slowly and take up a new position!

You might not want to cover yourself in paint, but if you support a team – a football or rugby club, for example – you might want to paint their colours on your face or hands. And if you visit a theme park, a show, a fete or other gathering, you might find someone who will paint your face to look like a bird or a butterfly or a tiger.

How would you like to be painted?

TAKE CARE! If you want to try painting your face or hands, you will need special paint that won't damage your skin. The paints you use on paper may hurt you – so make sure you have the right kind before you start.

In the story 'The Cheetah's Whisker' Abeba enjoys playing
tegre with her friends. Tegre is the Ethiopian name for a game
called mancala. Mancala is a very old game indeed – there's
evidence that it's 1,300 years old, but it may be far more
ancient than that (one archaeologist thought he had found
an ancient Egyptian mancala board carved into a piece of
limestone). It's played in different versions all over Africa
and in parts of Asia, and it has many different names. Most
versions are for two players.

It can be played using shallow holes scooped out of the
ground – or on beautifully carved and decorated boards.

This game is the version played by the Akan people of Ghana.
It is called oware, and is a very ancient form of mancala.

How to play:

You will need two rows of six holes, plus two containers for
storage such as saucers or small bowls. You could use an
empty box for 12 eggs as your holes, if you cut off the lid.
Your holes are the six in front of you.

You also need 48 playing pieces – large seeds, dried beans, small shells or pebbles could be used. These pieces are known as 'seeds'. Place four in each of the 12 holes.

The player who starts takes all four seeds out of one of the holes on their side of the board. Moving in an anti-clockwise direction (to the right!), they 'sow' the seeds by putting one in each hole.

When the last seed has been 'sown', this player picks up all the seeds in that hole, including the one they've just put there, and carries on 'sowing' the seeds. This continues until the last seed goes into an empty hole (unless you've made a mistake, this should mean you've lifted seeds five times).

Now the second player lifts seeds (or a seed) from any hole on their side, and sows them around the board, again working anti-clockwise.

After this first round, look at the holes on your side. If there are four seeds in any of them, scoop them up and put them in your storage bowl. You can do this even if your opponent is sowing seeds.

If you have four seeds in a hole when you put your last seed in it, and the hole is on your side of the board, the seeds are yours, so put them in your store. If you do this, your turn finishes.

If your opponent has four seeds on their side, they win the seeds and their turn finishes.

When there are only eight seeds left, the game is over. The eight seeds belong to the player who started the game.

For the second game, each player fills as many holes with four seeds as they can, and all those holes belong to them. The player who started second the first time round now begins to sow seeds into holes (starting turns alternate).

The game ends when one of the players can no longer put four seeds in a hole to start a game. The player with the most seeds wins.

Marimba, the mother of music, was good at inventing musical instruments. Here's one you could make for yourself.

You will need:

- Some empty jam jars – if you can find eight that are all the same shape and size, it is easier to make a scale, but you can use a range of jars
- A jug of water
- A metal spoon
- Newspaper to catch any drips or spills

What you do:

Put the newspaper on a flat surface, and arrange the jam jars on it in a row. Pour different amounts of water into each jar, from hardly any to quite full. Tap them with the spoon (gently!). You should get a different note from every jar – try arranging them with the highest note at one end and the lowest at the other. You might need to adjust the amounts of water (spoon a little out, pour a little in) to get a proper scale.

With a little practice, you should be able to play simple tunes on your glass xylophone.

Try tapping different parts of the jars. Is there a change in sound if you tap the top or the bottom?

FUL SUDANI – PEANUT SOUP

Peanuts grow in warm climates, and African farmers produce a large proportion of the world's crop. They are very good for you! That may be one reason why peanuts appear in a number of African recipes.

This peanut soup recipe comes from the Sudan, but there are many other versions from different African countries. There is enough soup here for six people, so you could cut the quantities in half if you don't need that much.

You will need:

- 450g (1lb) shelled peanuts
- 1 litre (1¾ pt) milk
- 1 litre (1¾ pt) chicken stock (you could use a stock cube)
- Salt and pepper
- Cream and butter, if you like

What you do:

Please ask an adult to help you before you begin.

Heat the oven to 180°C (350°F).

Spread the peanuts in a single layer on a baking tray, and roast in the oven for 15–20 minutes.

Leave to cool, then rub off their skins.

If you have a mincer or food processer, grind up the roasted peanuts. If you don't, you could crush them with a pestle and mortar, or put them in batches into a clean plastic bag, and squash them as finely as you can using a rolling pin. Be careful not to puncture the bag! You don't want to lose any peanuts – or have bits of plastic in your food.

When all the peanuts are finely crushed, put them in a mixing bowl. Add the milk slowly, stirring all the time. Then add the stock, still stirring. Add a little salt and pepper. Pour the whole mixture into a big saucepan. Cook over a moderate heat until the soup comes to the boil. Carry on cooking for 10 minutes, stirring often.

Before you serve the soup, add a little cream and butter, if you like.

GLOSSARY

addax – a large antelope found in the deserts of North Africa. Addaxes have greyish-white coats, and can go without water for long spells. They are a critically endangered species

afterbirth – the placenta and membranes that come from a mother's womb soon after she gives birth to her baby. They nourished the baby while it grew inside its mother, but aren't needed once it is born

atuu – a big hug

diviner – a person who seeks knowledge, particularly of the future, by magic or supernatural means

entrails – the inside organs of an animal

flay – to take the skin off a person or an animal

gourd – a large fruit with a hard skin. The dried skin can be used as a container for water

harmattan – a dry, dusty wind from the east that blows along coastal regions of West Africa

hyrax – a small plant-eating mammal with a thick fur coat and a short tail. Hyraxes live in small family groups in Africa south of the Sahara and in the Middle East. Although a hyrax looks something like a mouse or a rabbit, its closest relatives are elephants and dugongs (relatives of manatees)

Igboland – an area in south-east Nigeria where the Igbo people live. It is sometimes spelled 'Ibo'

impala – an antelope found in southern and eastern Africa. An impala has horns curved in the shape of a lyre, and a coat that is brown, black and white. Impalas like to live on the edges of woods and grasslands, and always near water

karimba – an African musical instrument in which tines – strips of metal of different lengths – are inserted into a piece of wood. When struck by thumb or finger, each tine makes a different note

makhoyana – a musical instrument made from a bow, like a hunting bow. When the taut string is picked, struck or rubbed by another bow, it makes a note. Sometimes a container, such as a gourd or a tin can, is added to the bow. This amplifies the sound

mentor – someone experienced at a skill or in a business, who can be trusted to train and advise students or new employees

perspective – how objects are seen, depending on their position and distance from the viewer

petrel – a seabird usually found far from land. Petrels fly close to the sea, trailing their feet, so it looks as if they are walking on the water!

quagga – a species of zebra, now extinct. The front half of a quagga's body had brown stripes on a yellowy white coat, and the back half was plain brown. Quaggas lived in South Africa, and were hunted until there were none left. London Zoo has the only photo of a live quagga, taken in 1870

tine – a prong. The prongs on a fork are called tines

trogon – a brightly coloured bird. Trogons live in tropical forests all over the world. There are three species of trogon that live in Africa. They nest in hollows which they make in trees and termite mounds

tropicbird – a large seabird, mostly white, with very long tail feathers, found in tropical waters. Their feet are set so far back on their bodies that they can't walk on land but have to push themselves along. They land to lay only one egg each year and raise their chick, which they feed so well that, when it fledges, it has to float on the water until it loses enough weight to be able to fly

Trou d'Eau Douce – a town on the east coast of Mauritius, which grew up at an important crossroads. It is named after the well of sweet water that was found there. Today it is a popular holiday resort

ululate – howling or wailing in grief